Also by Elizabeth Enright

THE MELENDY QUARTET

Thimble Summer

Written and Illustrated
by
Elizabeth Enright

Square Fish

HENRY HOLT

To My Mother

SQUARE
FISH
An Imprint of Macmillan

Library of Congress Cataloging-in-Publication Data
Enright, Elizabeth.
Thimble summer. Written and illustrated by Elizabeth Enright.
New York, Holt, Rinehart and Winston [1938]
I. Title PZ7.E724TH2 66-43350

ISBN 978-0-312-38002-1
Originally published in the United States by Henry Holt and Company
Square Fish logo designed by Filomena Tuosto
First Square Fish Edition: May 2008
10 9 8
mackids.com

AR: 5.7 / F&P: U / LEXILE: 810L

Contents

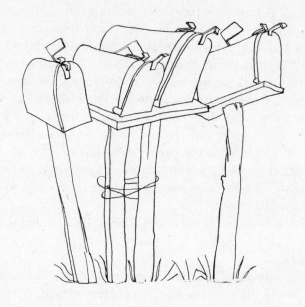

I. The Silver Thimble

GARNET thought this must be the hottest day that had ever been in the world. Every day for weeks she had thought the same thing, but this was really the worst of all. This morning the thermometer outside the village drug store had pointed a thin red finger to one hundred and ten degrees Fahrenheit.

It was like being inside of a drum. The sky like a bright skin was stretched tight above the valley, and the earth too, was tight and hard with heat. Later, when it was dark, there would be a noise of thunder, as though a great hand beat upon the drum; there would be heavy clouds above the hills, and flashes of heat lightning, but no rain. It had been like that for a long time. After supper each night her father came out of the house and looked up at the sky, then down at his fields of corn and oats. "No," he would say, shaking his head, "No rain tonight."

The oats were turning yellow before their time, and the corn leaves were torn and brittle, rustling like newspaper when the dry wind blew upon them. If the rain didn't come soon there would be no corn to harvest, and they would have to cut the oats for hay.

Garnet looked up at the smooth sky angrily, and shook her fist. "You!" she cried, "Why in time can't you let down a little rain!"

At each step her bare feet kicked up a small cloud of dust. There was dust in her hair, and up her nose, making it tickle.

Garnet was halfway between nine and ten. She had long legs and long arms, two taffy-colored pigtails, a freckled nose that turned up, and eyes that were almost green and almost brown. She wore a pair of blue overalls, cut off above the knee. She could whistle between her teeth like a boy and was doing it now, very softly, without thinking. She had forgotten all about her anger at the sky.

Under its big, black fir trees the Hausers' farm lay solid and sleepy-looking at the bend in the road. There was a bed of burning red salvia flowers on the lawn, and the tractor and threshing machine stood side by side in the shade, like friendly monsters. Across the road the Hauser pigs lay slumbering and wheezing under their shelter. "Lazy fat things," said Garnet, and threw a pebble at the biggest hog, who snorted horribly and lumbered to his feet. But Garnet just laughed at him; the fence was between them.

4

Behind her a screen door twanged shut, and Citronella Hauser came down the steps of her house flapping a dish towel like a fan. She was a fat little girl, with red cheeks and thick yellow bangs.

"Land!" she called to Garnet. "Isn't it hot! Where you going?"

"For the mail," said Garnet. "We might go swimming," she added thoughtfully.

But no. Citronella had to help her mother with the ironing. "A fine thing to have to do on a day like this," she said rather crossly. "I bet you I'll melt all over the kitchen floor like a pound and a half of butter."

Garnet giggled at this picture and started on her way.

"Wait a minute," said Citronella, "I might as well see if there's any mail for us too."

As she walked she did different things with the dish towel. First she draped it over her head like a shawl, then she tied it around her waist but it was too tight, and it ended up tucked in the back of her belt, hanging down behind like a train.

"Days like this," remarked Citronella, "make me wish I could find a waterfall somewhere. One that poured lemonade instead of water. I'd sit under it all day with my mouth open."

"I'd rather be up on an Alp," said Garnet. "You know, one of those mountains they have in Europe. There's snow on top of them even on the hottest days of summer. I'd like to be sitting in the snow looking miles and miles down into a valley."

"Too much trouble climbing up," sighed Citronella.

They turned the corner and kept along the highway till they came to the mailboxes. There were four of them set up on narrow posts. They were big tin boxes with curved tops, and some of them tilted crazily upon their pedestals. Always they made Garnet think of thin old women in crooked sunbonnets, gossiping beside the road.

Each box was named in black, stenciled letters. Hauser, Schoenbecker, Freebody and Linden.

The Hausers usually had the most mail because they were the largest family, and Citronella and her brothers were always sending for free samples of things advertised in papers. Today there was a small bottle of hair dye and a sample of hog mash for Citronella, as well as three different kinds of tooth paste for her brother Hugo.

They peeked into old Mr. Schoenbecker's box to see if the wren's nest was still there. It was, and had been for a year. There were never any letters.

Garnet opened the box marked Linden, which was her last name, and pulled out a bulky package.

"Look, Citronella," she cried, "here's the Merchant-Farmer's Catalogue."

Citronella grabbed it and tore off the paper wrapper. She and Garnet both loved to look at the catalogues from the big department store. In it there were pictures of everything in the world that you migh⁺ wish to buy, beside a lot of other things that you mightn't, like tractor parts and various kinds of hot-water bottles and pages and pages of union suits.

Garnet took the rest of the mail from her box. These weren't real letters, she could tell at a glance. The envelopes were thin and businesslike with small printed names of companies in upper left-hand corners, and two of them had long transparent windows in them. No, these weren't real letters. Bills, that's what they were.

Citronella was gazing at the picture of a beautiful young woman in an evening gown. Underneath the picture it said: " 'You're the top; a perfect dance frock. Sizes 14 to 40. $11.98' "

"When I am sixteen," said Citronella dreamily, *"all* my dresses are going to be like that."

But Garnet wasn't listening. Bills. She knew what that meant. Tonight her father would sit late in the kitchen, worried and silent, doing sums on a piece of paper. Long after everyone else had gone to bed, the lamp would burn and he would be there by himself. If it would only rain! Then there would be good crops and more money. She looked up at the sky. It was as smooth, as empty, as it had been for weeks.

"I've got to get back to my precious ironing board," said Citronella grimly, slapping the catalogue shut and handing it to Garnet.

They parted at the Hauser farm and Garnet couldn't help laughing at Citronella's fat back, with the dishtowel train switching after her.

As she walked up the long hill to her house she could see the glassy river between trees. It was getting lower and lower. Pretty soon it would be too low for anything but wading.

Drops of perspiration rolled down her forehead and into her eyes like big tears. Her back felt wet. She wished that she didn't have to give those bills to her father.

The shadows were getting longer when she turned in at the gate. Her brother Jay was bringing buckets of milk from the barn to the cold room under the house. He was eleven years old, tall for his age, and very dark.

"Any mail for me?" he called.

Garnet shook her head, and Jay went into the cold room.

The barn was huge and old; it lurched to one side like a

7

bus going round a corner. Some day, when he had enough money, her father was going to build a new one. There was a big silo beside the barn and Garnet thought again, as she often had, how nice it would be to have a room there; little and round, with a window opening outward on a hinge. It would be like a room in the tower of a castle.

She stopped for a moment beside the pigpen to look at Madam Queen, the big sow, and her litter of little ones. They were still quite new, with large silky ears and tiny hoofs that made them look as if they were wearing high-heeled slippers. Madam Queen rolled over like a tidal wave, scattering her squealing babies right and left. She was an impatient mother, grunting crossly, and kicking them off when they bothered her.

Garnet hadn't named the little pigs yet. She leaned against the rail and thought of names. The largest of the litter was unusually greedy and selfish even for a pig. He stepped on his brothers and nipped their ears and pushed them out of his way. Undoubtedly he would grow up to be a prize hog like his father. Rex might be a good name for him, or Emperor, or Tyrant; something with a large, bold sound to it. Garnet's favorite was the runt, a tiny, satiny pig with a sad face and no fighting spirit. He never got enough to eat. For some reason Timmy seemed the very name for him.

Slowly Garnet walked to the yellow house under tall maple trees and opened the kitchen door.

Her mother was cooking supper on the big black coal stove, and her little brother Donald sat on the floor making a noise like a train.

Her mother looked up. Her cheeks were red from the hot stove. "Any mail, darling?" she asked. "Bills," replied Garnet.

"Oh," said her mother and turned back to her cooking.

"And the catalogue from Merchant-Farmers," Garnet said quickly. "There's a dress in it that would look nice on you." She found the picture of "You're the top."

"I don't think it's quite my style, darling," laughed her mother looking at the dress, and softly pulling Garnet's left-hand pigtail.

Garnet set the table by the open window. Knife, fork, knife, fork, knife, fork, knife, fork but only a spoon for Donald, who managed even that so absent-mindedly that there was usually as much cereal on the outside of him as inside at the end of a meal.

In the middle of the table she put a bottle of catsup, salt and pepper, a china sugar bowl with morning-glories on it, and a tumbler-full of spoons. Then she went down to the cold room.

It was still and dim down there. A spigot dripped peacefully into the deep pool of water below, where the milk cans and stone butter crock were sunk. Garnet filled a pitcher with milk and put a square of butter on the plate she had brought. She knelt down and plunged both her arms into the water. It was cloudy with spilled milk but icy cold. She could feel coolness spreading through all her veins and a little shiver ran over her.

Going in the kitchen again was like walking into a red-hot oven.

Donald had stopped being a train and had become a fire engine. He charged round and round the room hooting and shrieking. How could he be so lively, Garnet wondered. He didn't even notice the awful heat although his hair clung to his head like wet feathers and his cheeks were red as radishes.

Her mother looked out of the window. "Father's

coming in," she said. "Garnet, don't give him the mail now, I want him to eat a good supper. Put it behind the calendar and I'll tend to it afterwards."

Garnet hastily pushed the bills behind the calendar on the shelf over the sink. There was a picture on the calendar of sheep grazing on a wild hillside with a vivid pink sky behind them. The name of it was Afterglow in the Highlands. Often Garnet looked at it and felt as though she were standing in that quiet place beside the sheep, hearing no sound but their grazing. It gave her a pleasant, far-off feeling.

The screen door opened with its own particular squeak and her father came in. He went to the sink and washed his hands. He looked tired and his neck was sunburned. "What a day!" he said. "one more like this — " and he shook his head.

It was too hot to eat. Garnet hated her cereal. Donald whined and upset his milk. Jay was the only one who really ate in a business-like manner, as if he enjoyed it. He could probably eat the shingles off a house if there was nothing else handy, Garnet decided.

After she had helped with the dishes, Garnet and Jay put on their bathing suits and went down to the river. They had to go down a road, through a pasture, and across half a dozen sand bars before they came to a place that was deep enough to swim in. This was a dark, quiet pool by a little island; trees hung over it and roots trailed in it. Three turtles slid from a log as the children approached, making three slowly widening circles on the still surface.

"It looks like tea," said Garnet, up to her neck in brownish lukewarm water.

"Feels like it too," said Jay. "I wish it was colder."

Still it was water and there was enough of it to swim in. They floated and raced and dove from the old birch tree bent like a bow over the pool. Jay dove very well, hardly making a splash when he entered the water, but Garnet landed flat on her stomach every time. As usual Jay cut his toe on a sharp stone and bled a great deal. As usual Garnet got caught in a swift current and had to be rescued, squealing, by Jay. With great care and trouble they built a raft out of dead branches that sank as soon as they both got on it. But nothing spoiled their fun.

When they were finally sufficiently waterlogged to be red-eyed and streaming, they went exploring on the sandy flats that had emerged from the river during the weeks of drought. There were all kinds of things to be found there; gaping clamshells colored inside like pearls; water-soaked branches with long beards of green moss; rusted tobacco tins, stranded fish, bottles, and a broken teapot.

They wandered in different directions, bending over, examining and picking things up. The damp flats had a rich, muddy smell. After a while the sun set brilliantly behind trees, but the air seemed no cooler.

Garnet saw a small object, half-buried in the sand, and glittering. She knelt down and dug it out with her finger. It was a silver thimble! How in the world had that ever found its way into the river? She dropped the old shoe, bits of polished glass, and a half dozen clamshells she had collected and ran breathlessly to show Jay.

"It's solid silver!" she shouted triumphantly, "and I think it must be magic too!"

"Magic!" said Jay. "Don't be silly, there isn't any such thing. I bet it's worth money, though." He looked a little envious. He had found two rather important things

11

himself — one was a ram's skull with moss growing out of the eye sockets, and the other was a big snapping turtle with a beak and a mean expression.

Garnet ran a finger gingerly over the turtle's beautifully marked shell.

"Let's call him Old Ironsides," she suggested. She liked naming things.

After a while it got too dark to see very well, and they went swimming again. Garnet held her thimble lightly. It was the best thing she had ever found and was sure to bring her luck, no matter what Jay said. She felt very happy and floated in the water, looking upwards into air that glittered with stars and fireflies.

As it grew darker the mosquitoes got very bad, and they decided to go home.

It was black and scary, sort of, coming back across the sand. All along the wooded banks owls hooted with a velvety, lost sound; and there was one that screamed, from time to time, in a high, terrifying voice. Garnet knew that they were only owls, but still, in the hot darkness with no light but the solemn winking of the fireflies, she felt that they *might* be anything; soft-footed animals, come alive with the night, watching and following among the trees. Jay didn't pay any attention to them. He slapped his towel at the mosquitoes.

"Listen, Garnet," he said suddenly, "when I grow up I'm not going to be a farmer."

"But, Jay, what else can you be?" asked Garnet, surprised.

"I don't want to be a farmer and watch my good crops eaten with wheat rust or dried up with drought. I don't want to spend my life waiting for weather. I want to be out in it. On the sea. I'd like to be a sailor."

Neither of them had ever seen the ocean but it had a

far wet, windy sound that excited them.

"I'll be one, too," she cried.

Jay just laughed at her. "You? Girls can't be sailors."

"*I* can be," replied Garnet firmly. "I'll be the first there ever was." And she saw herself in sailor pants, with stars on her collar, climbing up a tall rigging. There was blue, dizzy air above her, full of birds; blue, heaving water far below; and a vast wind blowing.

She was so absorbed with this picture that she forgot what she was doing and walked slam into the fence, catching her bathing suit on the barbed wire. "Crazy, why don't you look where you're going?" said Jay patiently, and unhooked her.

They rolled under the wire into the pasture. It was very dark, and they had to be careful where they stepped. The air was close and still.

"I don't feel like I've been swimming at all," Jay complained. "I'm hotter than I was before. For two cents I'd go back and take another dip."

"I wouldn't," said Garnet. "I want to go to bed." It made her feel creepy to think of swimming in the black river with all those owls carrying on. But she didn't tell Jay that.

The air smelled of dust and pasture flowers; pennyroyal, bee balm, and ladies' tobacco. Garnet sniffed it deeply.

"Let's only be sailors in wintertime," she said. "I want to spend all my summers here."

They climbed over the pasture gate, and walked up the powdery, dusty road to the house. A single lamp burned in the kitchen. Through the window they saw their father bent over a notebook.

"Doggone it!" whispered Jay. "I *won't* ever be a farmer!"

13

Garnet said goodnight and tiptoed up the stairs to her room under the eaves. It was so hot there that the candle in its holder had swooned till it was bent double. Garnet straightened it and lit it from the one she had brought upstairs. Moths saw the light and came to the window, banging softly against the screen, and climbing up and down it with quick, delicate legs. Tiny insects crawled through the screen's meshes and fluttered about the flames and burned themselves. Garnet blew out the candles and lay down. It was too hot even for a sheet. She lay there, wet with perspiration, feeling the heat like heavy blankets and listening to the soft thunder, the empty thunder, that brought no rain. After a while she fell asleep and dreamed that she was in a rowboat with Jay on a wide, flat ocean. She was rowing and it was hot work; her arms ached. Jay sat in the prow with a spy glass. "There's not a farmhouse in sight," he kept saying, "not a single one."

Late in the night Garnet woke up with a strange feeling that something was about to happen. She lay quite still, listening.

The thunder rumbled again, sounding much louder that it had earlier in the evening; almost as though it were in the earth instead of the sky, making the house tremble a little. And then slowly, one by one, as if someone were dropping pennies on the roof, came the raindrops. Garnet held her breath: the sound paused. "Don't stop!" she whispered. A noise of wind stirred in the leaves, and then the rain burst strong and loud upon the world. Garnet leaped out of bed and ran to the window. The watery air was cold against her face and as she looked the many-branched lightning stood for an instant on the horizon like a tree on fire.

Quickly she turned and ran down the little stairway

to her father's and mother's bedroom. Loudly she banged upon the door and threw it open, calling, "It's raining! It's raining hard!" She felt as though the thunderstorm were a present she was giving to them.

Her father and mother got up and went to the windows. They could hardly believe it. But it was true. The sound of rain was everywhere, and when the lightning came you could see it, heavy and silver as a waterfall.

Garnet flew down the next flight of stairs and out of doors. In five minutes the world had changed to a violent, unfamiliar place. The thunder was like big drums, like cannons, like the Fourth of July, only louder. The rain was like a sea turned upside down; and the wind blew hugely, tossing the trees and making their branches creak. In the flashes of bright lightning Garnet saw the horses in the lower pasture, their heads raised and manes blowing. Even they seemed different.

In the house she heard her mother closing windows; quickly she ran to Jay's window and called to him; "Wake up, wake up! Come on out and get wet!" Her brother's astonished face appeared. "Oh boy!" he said and in less than a second was out of doors.

Squealing and yelling they ran round and round the lawn like wild animals. Garnet stubbed her toe and fell headlong into the rhubarb bed, but she didn't care. She had never been happier in her life. Jay grabbed her by the hand and they ran down the slope and through the vegetable garden. They slipped and slid, dodged bean poles and hurdled cabbages, and landed exhausted at the pasture fence.

Suddenly the air blazed with a light so brilliant that Garnet shut her eyes. At the same second there was a noise as if the world had split in two; the ground shook under their feet. That meant the lightning had struck somewhere near by. Too near for Garnet. She heard her mother calling from the doorway and ran like a rabbit to the house.

"We were Comanche Indians doing a rain dance," she explained.

"You're soaking!" cried her mother. "You're filthy, both of you, and you'll probably catch your death of cold." But above the lamp she held her face was smiling and she said, "I declare, I wouldn't mind doing the same thing myself."

It was cool in the house now. The wind blew the curtains into Garnet's room. She put on a dry nightgown, pulled the blanket up under her chin, and listened to the storm. For a long time it boomed and crashed and glittered, then by degrees the thunder and lightning grew less and less and disappeared entirely.

But all night long the rain fell steadily with a sound of gutters running, eaves dripping, wet leaves slapping together, water coming through a leak in the attic and dropping into a dishpan, ping-ping-ping, like someone beating a little gong.

When Garnet held her breath and listened very carefully, it almost seemed as if she could hear roots deep in the wet earth drinking and coming to life again.

II. The Coral Bracelet

IT WAS raining hard one afternoon several days later when Garnet went to get the mail. She wore a slicker that was too short for her, and a pair of Jay's rubber boots that were too big and made a slumph, slumph noise at every step.

The road streamed with little rivers the color of coffee and cream. Tiny toads hopped about and Garnet walked carefully so as not to step on them. Her slicker had a strong oily smell that was delicious, and she had found a forgotten piece of licorice in one of the pockets.

In the mailbox there was an important looking envelope for her father, two letters for her mother and an uninteresting postal card for Jay on which there was a picture of an office building and two parked cars. It was from Uncle Julius in Duluth. There weren't any letters for Garnet, but then there never were except at Christmas time and on her birthday.

She put the mail in her sticky slicker pocket and turned back towards Citronella's house. She slopped and splashed across the lawn and up the porch steps and looked through the screen door at the dark hall with the hat rack and rubber plant.

"Citro-nella!" she called and pressed her face against the screen. The Hauser house had its own smell like all houses. It smelled of brown soap and ironing and linoleum; rather stuffy.

"Citronella!" called Garnet again and this time Citronella answered and came thumping down the stairs, with her bangs flopping on her forehead.

"I was up in great-grandma's room," she explained. "Come on up, Garnet. She's telling me about when she was little."

Garnet stepped out of her muddy boots and went in. She hung her slicker up and barefooted climbed the stairs behind Citronella.

Citronella's great-grandmother was named Mrs. Eberhardt, and she was very, very old. She had a little room in the front of the house, full of photographs of her relatives. She had grown small with age and sat, light as a leaf, in a rocking chair with a red crocheted blanket over her knees. She liked bright colors, and especially red.

"Yes," she told the two children, "I always liked red. When I was a little girl we used to make our own dye for clothes. In the fall we gathered the sumach berries and boiled them; then we'd dip in the cloth, but when it was finished it came out sort of a brownish color, not the red you'd expect. I was always disappointed."

"What was it like then, in this valley?" asked Garnet.

"Oh, it was wild country," replied Mrs. Eberhardt. "There was only one other family living there. Blaiseville was the nearest town, three miles away, and it was a little bit of a place then. We used to work very hard, we had to do everything for ourselves. There were eleven of us children; I was next to the youngest. The boys helped father plowing and tending the farm, and the girls helped mother with the churning, baking, spinning and soap-making. In summer, when we were tiny things, we used to lie in my father's wheat field, each with a pair of shingles to slap together when the crows came over. The deer sometimes came too, and we had to frighten them away. But often we used to go down to the river and hide in the bushes and watch them come to drink. Beautiful animals they were, but I haven't seen one in thirty years.

"Yes, it was wild country then, all woods and open fields and very few roads. My father used to ride into Blaiseville on a chestnut mare named Duchess. Sometimes when I was good he'd take me too, riding behind him and holding to his waist. My, my, he was a big man. It was like putting your arms around a big tree. Often we wouldn't start home till after dark, and it used to make me feel important and sort of adventurous to be riding through those thick, black woods with my father.

"There were Indians, too, in those days. I used to sleep in a little trundle bed with my sister Matty. In the daytime it was pushed under the big bed my father and mother slept in, but at night it was pulled out and set in its own corner. From where we lay we could see into the next room where the fire was burning. My, we had awful winters then. We used to be snowbound for weeks at a time. We kept the fires burning day and night and I remember wearing three pairs of woolen knit stockings and so many flannel petticoats I must have looked like a cabbage wrong-side up. Well, on those cold nights when Matty and I were supposed to be asleep we'd sometimes look into the other room where the shadows and firelight kept changing shape and flickering, and then suddenly we'd see the front door begin to open. 'Look Matty,' I'd whisper and pinch her. 'They're coming in again.' I felt sort of scared with goose flesh all over me, and Matty'd grab my hand. Sure enough, the door would open wide and in would come the Indians, quiet as cats, sometimes one or two, sometimes as many as ten. They wore fur hats and clothes made out of deerskin. We could hear them grunt and sigh as they lay down in front of the fire in our warm house. We never saw them leave, we were asleep, and they went out very early before it was light; but we'd always find a present left behind in exchange for our fireside. Sometimes it was a haunch of venison, or a couple of rabbits for stewing, or maybe a basket, or a sack of meal. Once I remember they left some moccasins and among them was a child's pair just my size. My, they were comfortable, and real pretty too, with bead work on the toes. I felt like crying when they wore out."

"I wish I had some," said Garnet, wriggling her bare toes. "They're the only kind of shoes I'd like to wear."

21

Citronella was lying on the floor tickling the Maltese cat who sat smiling with his paws folded under him and purring roughly.

"Tell me about the time you were bad, great-grandma," said Citronella. "You know, on your tenth birthday."

Mrs. Eberhardt laughed. "Again?" she asked. "Well, Garnet hasn't heard it, has she? You know, Garnet, I was a very headstrong child, always wanting my own way and flying into tantrums when I was crossed. Well, in Blaiseville at that time there was only one store; a general store it was — "

"It was called Elly Gensler's Emporium," interrupted Citronella, who knew the story by heart.

"Yes," said Mrs. Eberhardt, "so it was. Elly Gensler was a tall, thin man without a chin, but we all liked him because he was good to us, and used to give us candy whenever we came in. He had everything in his store that you could think of: harness, groceries, calico by the yard, candy, shoes, books, tools, hats, grain and feed, and jewelry and toys. It was a wonderful place. My father used to joke about it. 'Elly,' he'd say, 'when you going to start selling livestock and locomotives?'

"Well, in Elly's showcase there was a coral bracelet, imitation I suppose it was, but my, I thought it was the prettiest thing I'd ever seen. It was made of coral beads with a coral heart dangling from it. I wanted it more than anything in the world; the only jewelry I'd ever had was strings of mountain ash berries, and rosehips. I thought about that bracelet and I thought about it; everytime I went to Blaiseville I was half scared to go in Elly's store for fear it had been sold. Finally Elly said to me, 'Well, that bracelet's worth a dollar; but since you want it so bad and it's been in stock so long I'll knock it down to you for fifty cents.'

" 'Oh, thank you, Elly,' said I. 'When I have fifty cents I'll come and get it.'

"That was early in May, and it wasn't till the end of August that I had enough money. I'd had about fifteen cents already in a china savings bank (it was blue and white I remember, and shaped like a wooden shoe), and I worked hard and did extra chores to earn more. I used to weed and tend the whole watermelon patch myself and my father would give me a penny on every melon he sold. My birthday was on the twenty-seventh of August and my father promised me that when it came he would take me to Blaiseville on Duchess and I could get the bracelet.

"Well, the birthday came at last, one of those clear, hot days that come towards the end of summer. I can remember it as if it was last week. I was ten years old. After breakfast I did my chores around the house and then I went out of doors. My father was saddling Duchess in front of the barn. My, I felt happy. I had the fifty cents tied up in a handkerchief that clinked when I shook it.

" 'Shall I change my dress, father?' I called.

"My father looked at me. 'Not today, Fanny,' he said. 'I can't take you today after all. I have to go to Hodgeville on business.'

"Well, I didn't say anything. I turned around and went into the house. I helped my mother and sisters with the washing, got vegetables from the garden for dinner, helped prepare and cook them. But I couldn't eat. All the time my anger was growing inside of me till I felt as if I'd burst. After dinner my brother Thomas and I went up to the woods with a couple of pails to get blackberries. I was getting madder and madder; tears kept coming into my eyes and I didn't see what I was doing and tore my dress on the brambles. Finally I couldn't stand it any longer. I gave Thomas my pail.

" 'You fill it,' I said. 'I'm going to Blaiseville to get my bracelet.'

"Thomas looked at me with his eyes popping. 'How you going to get there?' he asked.

" 'Walk,' said I, 'and if you tell anybody where I've gone I'll whip you good!'

"Poor Thomas, his mouth hung open; he was only six years old. I should have known better than to leave him there alone! But I was a naughty, heedless girl.

"Well, so I walked and walked. It was hot and the road was dusty and I got a blister on my heel. But with every step the money in my pocket thumped against my leg and I thought about the bracelet. Finally I got to Blaiseville and walked straight into Elly Gensler's store.

" 'I've come for the bracelet, Elly,' said I. 'I've got fifty cents to buy it with.'

"Elly looked at me kind of queer. 'Why, Fanny,' said he, 'I thought you wasn't never coming. I sold that bracelet to Minetta Harvey more'n a week ago.'

"Well, that was just too much. I put my head down on the counter and cried fit to break my heart. Elly felt real bad about it.

" 'Now, Fanny,' he said, 'don't cry. I'll sell you the little agate locket for the same price and it's a better buy. Or maybe you'd like to have the blue bead necklace?'

"But, no, nothing would do for me except that coral bracelet.

"At last I stopped crying and dried my eyes and told

Elly I had to go as it was getting late. I don't suppose he had any idea I was going home alone at that hour, or he wouldn't have let me leave. He gave me an all-day sucker and patted my shoulder.

" 'Never mind about that little bracelet,' he said. 'Next time I go to Hodgeville maybe I can find you another one just like it.'

"Well, the sun was setting and I commenced to hurry. The woods were dark and thick on either side of the road and they got darker by the minute. There wasn't any sound except the crickets. I sniffled some, and felt sorry for myself. My, but I was disappointed and tired too.

"I'd gone about three quarters of the way, I guess, when I noted that someone was walking towards me on the road. It was real dark by this time, the stars were out but it was hard to see. For a minute I thought of hiding by the roadside, but then I decided that since I knew every single person for miles around, there was nothing to be scared of. It wasn't till I got close to him that I saw this man was a stranger. He had a bundle under one arm and he was wearing a deerskin jacket like the Indians wore.

" 'Good evening,' said I politely as I came near to him. I kept right on going.

" 'Hello, little girl,' said the man and reached out and grabbed me by the arm. 'Where are you going in such a hurry?'

" 'Home,' I answered, trying not to sound scared. 'Please let me go, I'm late for supper.' Oh dear, oh dear, I thought, why didn't I stay with Thomas?

" 'Supper,' said the man. 'How would you like it if you didn't have any supper to go to? How would you like it if you didn't know where your next meal was coming from?' He held my arm tighter. 'Or have you perhaps got a few pennies in your pocket that will buy some food for a hungry man?'

" 'Oh, yes, yes!' I cried and I took the knotted handkerchief out of my pocket and gave it to him. 'There's fifty cents there,' I said, 'and you can keep it all.' Then I pulled my arm free and ran like the wind. I didn't dare look back, but it seemed to me as if I could hear that man laughing at me all the way home.

"I stumbled up the path to our door and burst into the house gasping for breath and red in the face.

" 'Fanny!' cried my mother, 'where is Thomas?'

" 'Thomas!' I said. 'Isn't he home?'

" 'Indeed he's not,' answered my mother. 'I've been sick with worry about you both; the boys were just going out to search for you. Where is Thomas? Where did you lose him?'

" 'Oh, mother,' I said, 'I left him getting blackberries all by himself.' Then I broke down and told her the whole story.

"My big brothers, Jonathan and Charles, went hunting for Thomas with a couple of lanterns. Charles took his shot-gun too.

"I went outside and sat on the gatepost looking out over the valley. By and by the moon came up. It was full, I remember, a real harvest moon; and the mists began to rise from the river and all the little ponds like smoke. An owl called and called somewhere in the woods and I heard a fox bark. I don't suppose there was a more miserable child in all the world than I was at that minute. Oh, Thomas, I thought, why did I leave you alone in the woods? And all for a silly bracelet that I never got.

27

"It seemed to me as if I sat there for hours. By the time I saw my brothers' lanterns glittering among the trees my clothes were drenched with dew and my teeth were chattering.

"My mother came out of the house and called to them: 'Is Thomas with you?'

"And he was, thank goodness! They'd found him wandering around and crying in that boggy place over near where Craddock's farm is now. All the time that he was lost and frightened he had been careful not to spill the blackberries out of the buckets!

"Well, I crept indoors and got undressed and into the trundle bed beside Matty who was fast asleep. A long while later I heard Duchess's hoofs on the wooden bridge over the slough and knew that my father was coming home from Hodgeville. That bridge always made a noise like thunder.

"When he came in I listened to my mother telling him about how I had behaved.

" 'Well, poor Fanny,' he said. 'I won't say anything further to her. She seems to have been punishing herself all day long.'

"And it was true. I felt just as if I'd had a whipping.

"So that's the story of what happened to me on my tenth birthday."

Garnet stood up and hopped on one foot. It was all pins and needles and she hadn't even noticed.

"Oh, I *wish* you'd gotten the bracelet," she said. "It's the worst birthday I ever heard of; I think your father was mean not to keep his promise."

"No, he was never mean," said Mrs. Eberhardt. "On the Christmas after that he gave me a little box, and what do you suppose was in it?"

"*I* know," gloated Citronella. "A coral bracelet was in it!" said her great-grandmother triumphantly. "The very twin of the one Elly had sold to Minetta Harvey. I could hardly believe my eyes. 'Father,' I shouted. 'where did you ever get it?' And, do you know, my father had bought that bracelet in Hodgeville on my birthday so many weeks before. It had caught his eye in a shop window, and he'd thought to himself 'There's a bracelet just like the one that Fanny wants so much. I'll get her this and she can keep her fifty cents for something else.' But of course when he got home and heard about all the trouble I'd caused he decided he'd better wait until Christmas."

"Have you got the bracelet still?" asked Garnet.

"No, not now," replied Mrs. Eberhardt. "I wore it till I was quite a big girl and then one day when I was drawing water from the well I reached out to take the bucket from the windlass and my bracelet broke apart. All the beads and the little red heart went tumbling into the water far below. I could hear them splash as they went in."

She gave a long sigh that ended in a yawn.

"Run along, children," she said, "I think I need a little nap now. It makes me sleepy to think so far back; more than seventy years ago, think of that. Was I the same person? Sometimes it seems as if it had all happened to somebody else."

Garnet and Citronella tiptoed down the stairs.

"I wish I had a great-grandmother," said Garnet enviously. "I've only got a grandmother, and she lives way off in Duluth so I never see her."

"Grant-grandma's nice," said Citronella complacently. "She tells me lots of stories. Only she *sleeps* all the time.

29

Old people always do, I wonder why. When I grow up I'm going to stay up all night long every night until I die."

The two girls went into the kitchen for something to eat. They found a chocolate cake in the cakebox and some hermits in a crockery jar. That was the wonderful thing about Citronella's house; there was always a cake in the kitchen at the right time. Often there was a dish of vinegar candy, too; and the cooky jar was never quite empty. Probably that was why most of the Hausers were so fat.

When Garnet said good-bye and went outdoors again she found that the rain had stopped and the afternoon sun was shining through a yellow mist. Clear drops of water hung from every leaf and petal, and mourning doves cried softly from all the woods in the valley. Garnet saw a snake move like a drawn ribbon through wet ferns; she saw a caterpillar with dewy fur climbing a mullein stalk, and a snail with his horns out enjoying the damp.

Once on days like this, thought Garnet, only the Indians had been here to see the snake, the caterpillar and the snail. On moccasined feet they had moved softly among the grasses and jostled down the rain drops from the elder flowers.

It would have been fun to be an Indian girl wearing a fringed deerskin dress. Garnet saw a long, rather bedraggled crow's feather in the grass and picked it up and stuck it in her hair. Then she crouched down and walked tiptoe in the way she imagined an Indian would walk.

A loud laugh startled her, and she looked up to see Jay leaning over the pasture fence.

"What are you walking all bent over like that for? And why have you got that old feather in your hair?" he asked. "You look like a hen with a stomach ache."

Garnet felt silly. She took the feather out of her hair and decided not to give Jay the postal card till later.

Then she went on to the barn where her father was and gave him the important looking letter. She wanted to know what was in it and leaned against a convenient cow while he opened it. He tore off the end of the envelope in a hurry, and she watched his eyes move swiftly back and forth over the printed lines of the letter. He smiled.

"Garnet," he said. "We won't have to worry any longer about having this old barn collapse over our heads. We're going to build a new one. The government's going to loan us some money!"

III. The Lime Kiln

GARNET yawned and slapped the lid on the last ham sandwich and put it with the others in a damp towel. She closed her mouth abruptly, remembering that this was no time to be yawning if she was going to stay up all night. She looked out of the window; already the swallows were high in the sky, always a sign of late afternoon; and she saw Jay in the pasture, carrying milk buckets.

Garnet stretched her arms above her head; up and up till all her muscles felt like pulled elastic. Then she took down the coffeepot; the big agate one with the chipped lid. It took plenty of coffee to keep her father awake on kiln nights.

At last the lime kiln was being fired; for three days and three nights it had burned steadily to make the lime needed in building a fine new barn — lime for cement, for plaster and for whitewash. The kiln was two miles away in a thick wood; it was a big cone-shaped oven, backed against a hill. Two of the Hausers' oldest boys stayed there all day pushing logs into the blazing fire, and in the evening — Garnet's father and Mr. Freebody relieved them. The fire had to be fed every ten or fifteen minutes, without fail, and the huge logs must be pushed in gently, so as not to jar the piled limestone structure within. Each night Garnet had begged to be taken along, and now at last her father had consented.

She put the big coffeepot on the table beside the other things, where it dominated the group like a brigadier general. Most kitchen articles had characters for Garnet. The teapot smiled all around its lid and purred like a kitten; the alarm clock stood with feet apart and wore its little gong like a cap on top; and Garnet often felt that the stove was a huge old woman waiting for her to make mistakes, and hissing scornfully when things boiled over.

She hummed softly and her voice sounded strange to her; the house was very quiet. Her father was asleep upstairs, and had been since this morning when he had returned, tired and grimy from the kiln. Her mother and Donald had gone down to the river for a cool breath of air and Jay was milking in the pasture since there was no longer any barn for the cows.

Garnet took an apple pie out of the cakebox and wrapped it in waxed paper: it was going to be fun to stay up all night. She didn't intend to sleep for a minute, even though her mother insisted on her taking some blankets along, just in case. At midnight she would heat the coffee, and they would all have a picnic.

Jay came into the kitchen whistling. "I'm going to

feed the hogs," said he, and picked up the covered bucket and swung out again. A moment later Garnet heard the pigs screaming like banshees in eagerness and greed.

Garnet had a special little dish filled with all the best scraps for Timmy; she picked it up and ran out-of-doors toward the pigpen. Timmy had grown wise and was waiting for her by the railing instead of fighting for food with his rude family. He was a much better looking pig now, since Garnet's care, and grunted with pleasure when he saw her; Garnet hoped he was glad to see her, too, as well as his dinner. She watched him gobble up the scraps, his ears trembling with enthusiasm, and one delicate hoof planted in the middle of the dish.

"When winter comes I'm going to give you cod-liver oil every day," she told him, "and by next summer I bet you'll be a very handsome hog. Maybe you'll win a ribbon at the fair."

Timmy turned away from the empty dish and lay down in a cool mud puddle with a snore of satisfaction, and Garnet went back to the house.

It seemed queer not to see the old, lopsided barn in its place. Last week her father and Jay and Mr. Freebody had torn it apart, and when nothing was left but the framework of the building her father had tied a strong rope to one of the posts and attached the other end to the tractor. Then he had driven the tractor hard till the framework collapsed with a tremendous crash, and the dust lifted in a yellow cloud.

Where the barn's red walls had risen, one now could see across the orchard and pastures to the river; piles of lumber and limestone from the quarry stood where it had been. As soon as the lime was ready they would start to build.

Garnet glanced at the clock; it was nearly six, and time to begin supper. She put more wood in the stove and filled the fat kettle with water. Then she went down to the garden with a basket to get some lettuce and cucumbers.

After the frequent rains the garden was fresh and flourishing. The watermelons in their patch were little green whales in a sea of frothy leaves, and the corn on the hillside was like a parade advancing with plumes and banners.

Garnet privately thought that vegetables in flower were as pretty as any garden plants. Okra had a creamy blossom with a dark red center like a hollyhock, the eggplants were starred with purple; gone-to-seed onions were topped with globes of lacy bloom, and each squash vine, vivid as a jungle growth, spread dark leaves above enormous orange flowers.

Garnet knelt to cut lettuces with a knife and laughed when a big toad hopped sulkily away. She got cucumbers, too, and as she started up the hill she met her mother and Donald returning from the river.

Donald's sun-suit was black where he had sat down in the mud. He carried a little fishing rod over his shoulder, but he had no fish.

"And no wonder," said their mother. "He was so busy pulling up the hook to see if there was anything on it that the fish didn't have time to bite."

"Next time I will take a gun and shoot them dead," said Donald darkly; and he banged and boomed at the top of his lungs all the way up to the house.

After supper Jay and Garnet said good-bye to their mother, and with their father got into the Ford car which had been in the family since Jay was a baby; it

35

was very high and narrow and elderly looking. Riding in it was rather like being on a throne, and rather like being in a motor boat. It rattled and chugged along the road at fifteen miles an hour, and sounded as if it were going fifty.

Both the children sat in the front seat with their father; picnic things, blankets and coats were piled in back.

The valley was filled with the blue color of dusk, and lamps in farmhouse windows burned with a clean white light.

There were hundreds of odors in the night air; Garnet raised her nose like a puppy to smell them all. Cabbages decaying richly in gardens made her hold her breath in passing; but the cornfields were wonderful, they had a special smell after dark that you never noticed in the daytime. It didn't smell like corn at all, but strange and spicy like incense in a church. Bouncing bet growing in ditches by the roadside gleamed pale in the dusk, and sent forth a sharp, sweet fragrance.

Garnet felt adventurous and happy. She had never spent a night away from home before, though Jay had been to Milwaukee twice and once to Chicago.

They turned from the highway along a rutted dirt road. The Ford thumped and jerked and quivered; in back the coffeepot's lid jingled like a tambourine. There were woods on either side of them now, and leaves meeting high above shut out the last of the light. Suddenly the air was close and dark.

Soon they saw the bright flicker of the kiln between trees. "Good!" said their father, "the fire has broken and this will be the last night I'll have to come here."

They stopped at the edge of a clearing and got out.

36

Mr. Freebody's old truck and the Hausers' newer one were parked near by.

The Hauser boys, Cicero and Merle, came running to meet them. Their faces were streaked with ash and they looked tired.

"Gee, we're glad to see you," said Cicero. "It's been mighty hot up here all day. But she's done a good job for us this time."

They got into the truck and called good night.

Garnet stared fascinated at the kiln. The huge oven, open at the top, was crowned with flames of white and purple, and the iron door was red-hot, and glowing like the eye of a dragon.

"See, Garnet," explained her father, "when the fire has reached its hottest pitch and the limestone in the oven is thoroughly cooked, the flame comes out of the top like that. That's what we mean when we say it's broken through."

Mr. Freebody was sitting on a log reading a paper. He was a small, quiet man with a big, fierce mustache which looked, even when he slept, as though it were awake and keeping watch. His dog, Major, lay dozing at his feet, twitching as he chased imaginary rabbits.

Every ten or fifteen minutes the two men slid open the metal door with a piece of lead pipe; the clanging sound shattered all the dark gathered stillness of the woods. For a few moments you could look into the brilliant heart of the fire as Mr. Freebody and Mr. Linden, staggering a little, lifted the big logs to feed it.

Garnet was enjoying this. She spread the blankets under a large chokecherry tree some distance from the fire. She arranged the picnic things, hanging cups on the twigs of a bush, and burying potatoes in hot wood ash raked from the kiln.

Jay was busy too. He helped the men with the logs, and slid open the glowing door for them.

Now and then people from neighboring farms, who had seen the flaming kiln in the woods, came to watch and talk for a while. Henry Jones, the old stonemason, came too. He had lived in the valley for eighty years, and could still remember the boat with big sails that had brought him and his family across the sea from Liverpool. He could remember, too, the wagon drawn by mules in which they had traveled to this valley where his father had settled. His father had taught his trade to Henry, who grew up to be the best stonemason in the county. But now he was very old. He sat on a tree stump half asleep and watched the kiln's bright crown.

"Seems like I've seen a thousand of them things burning in my life," he told Garnet.

By-and-by as it grew late, the people went away and just the four of them were left. Five, if you counted Major.

Garnet sat on a blanket under the chokecherry tree and watched Jay and the two men refuelling the fire. Beyond this circle of light and sound the woods spread, seeming taller and more wild than in the day. How still it was! And yet not really still at all when she listened closely. There were dozens of sounds: hoots of owls, stirring of leaves, a whippoorwill in some distant swamp who talked and talked as if he could never stop. And everywhere, overhead, underfoot and in the air beside her, she heard insects making their tiny noises. But all these sounds together made a sort of stillness.

Garnet thought: "I will just lie down for a minute, but I won't go to sleep."

Between feathery branches she watched the stars.

Suddenly one of them shot across the sky with a tail of flame; she made a wish on it. And then in spite of herself her eyes closed and she slept.

The loud clattering of the kiln door wakened her. In the silence that followed she sat up and rubbed her eyes and heard the clock in the Blaiseville courthouse miles away ringing the hour. She counted the strikes; there were twelve of them — clear and perfect on the air. She had never been awake before to hear the clock strike twelve at night!

She got up, put coffee and water in the big pot and climbed the narrow path on the hillside to the top of the kiln. She set the pot on the coals as near the crown of flames as she could get.

When she came down she raked the potatoes out of the ash; they were well roasted now and their coats were black.

Jay had a beard of soot. "Gosh, I'm hungry," he said.

"I am, too," agreed Garnet. "I never ate a meal at midnight before." Food should have a special taste at such an hour, she thought.

When the coffee was done she put it on a paper with the lopsided ham sandwiches. Nobody said much. They just sat in the flickering light and ate everything. There was hardly a crumb left.

When Garnet brought out the apple pie Mr. Freebody pretended to faint.

"More food!" he groaned. "I couldn't touch a mouthfull." But he ate two slices just the same.

Afterwards Garnet settled down under the tree again. The dew was falling, and she pulled a blanket over her; it smelled faintly of frying for some reason, and of camphor. Her father and Mr. Freebody were talking in grown-up voices about things like politics and the price of feed; Jay, trying not to look sleepy, sat on a log in the firelight pretending to listen as he whittled a stick.

Suddenly Major growled. He had not made a sound all evening, and had behaved very well, only showing a natural anxiety about the ham sandwiches.

But now he stood staring into a dark thicket and growling with the hair rising on his neck. It was an ugly sound.

IV. The Stranger

WHAT do you see, Major?" asked Mr. Freebody. "What is it, a skunk?"

They all looked towards the shadowy place that Major was watching so intently.

There was a sound then, of leaves stirring and twigs breaking. What could be coming out of these dark woods so late at night? Garnet felt gooseflesh all over her skin. For a minute she wished that she was at home, safe in her own bed.

Major's growl ended in a burst of terrified, defiant barking. He dashed forward and Mr. Freebody sprang to his feet as the bushes parted and someone emerged.

Garnet's racing heart turned over in relief. Why this was only a boy, hardly older than Jay, and certainly nobody to be afraid of.

"Be quiet, Major," said Mr. Freebody. "Where do you come from, boy?" he asked the newcomer.

There was something the matter with the boy. He walked crookedly and suddenly lurched forward, half falling to the ground.

"Excuse me," he said. Then he looked up at the surprised faces surrounding him and grinned.

"I smelled coffee. I bet it was a mile away! And I just followed my nose till I got here. Gee, and when I saw that oven of yours I thought the whole woods was on fire." He licked his lips nervously. "Do you think — would it be all right — I mean could I have some coffee, please?"

Garnet didn't know that boys ever drank coffee but she ran to get him some.

"How long since you et, boy?" she heard Mr. Freebody asking.

And she heard the reply: "Day before yesterday."

"My gosh!" said Jay's horrified voice at her elbow. "Two days! Give him some pie for Pete's sake. And aren't there any sandwiches left?"

"You ate four of them yourself, if you think back," Garnet reminded him. "And Major cleaned up the crumbs. But he can have some potatoes and a slice of pie, anyway."

Jay was shaking his head. "Gee whiz! Two whole days without anything to eat!" He couldn't imagine such a thing; he who had always thought three meals a day about half as many as a person needed.

The boy ate everything that was offered him and

drank the strong black coffee eagerly. When he had finished he smiled again. "I guess I'll live now."

Garnet's father began asking questions. "How old are you?" he said.

"Thirteen," answered the boy, "but I pass for fifteen when I want to."

"What are you doing in these woods at this time of night?" asked her father.

"Yes, and where do you come from? I never seen you before," added Mr. Freebody sternly.

"I was hitchhiking," said the boy. "This afternoon I couldn't get a ride on anything but a hay wagon. I was kind of dizzy from being hungry, I guess, and the hay was so swell and soft that I went to sleep and woke up way off in the backwoods somewhere. The fellow had unhitched the team in the barn and forgotten all about me. Well, it was night by that time, and when I knocked at the door of this fellow's house, I woke him up and he was kind of sore, so I didn't ask him for anything to eat. He told me to cut through the woods and I'd get back to the highway. I thought maybe I could hop a ride on a truck; there are lots of them on the road at night. But I got lost, and then I smelled coffee and all I could think of was getting to the place where the smell came from."

"Have more," said Garnet.

"No thanks," said the boy. "I ought to be getting along. I want to catch a truck. Thanks a lot for the food." He stood up.

"Just a minute," said Garnet's father. "I think perhaps you'd better tell us a little more about yourself first. Maybe we can help you."

A shadow seemed to pass over the boy's face. You

could see that he didn't want to talk about himself, but he sat down again.

"What's your name?" asked Mr. Freebody.

"Eric Swanstrom," answered the boy, and closed his mouth firmly.

"Where are your folks?" persisted Mr. Freebody.

"Haven't any," said Eric, "or if I have I don't know where they are." He looked up. "I'm by myself and I get along all right the way I am. I don't want people thinking they have to look out for me, and I don't want to go to an orphanage. I've taken care of myself for a year and I don't see why I can't for the rest of my life. I like it."

"All right, all right," said Mr. Freebody. "But we're entitled to a little information from an unknown boy who walks out of the woods in the middle of the night and eats up all the apple pie we got!"

Eric sighed and reluctantly began to speak.

"My people came from Sweden," he said. "My mother died when I was a year old, and my father took care of me from then on. He bought a little farm out in Minnesota. It was nice there, I can still remember it: big trees and stuff. There was a brook to wade in and we had three cows and a couple of goats, and we got along all right till one day my father fell on a pitchfork and hurt his hand. He got blood poisoning after that and he was too sick to walk the five miles into town to the doctor. I was only a kid of four so I couldn't either. We didn't have a telephone. Finally my father sent me to the nearest farmhouse and the folks there went and got the doctor. It was too late then though and my father lost his arm. After that he couldn't do farm work and we sold the place and moved to New York; he thought there'd be more chances there for a crippled man. He bought a newspaper-stand concession. It was a little shed like a box, with one side open and a sort of shelf in front with newspapers on it, and boxes of chocolate bars and chewing gum; things like that. We sold magazines too, and my father always wanted to get a bigger place and sell ginger ale and Coca-Cola in summer time. I used to help him there when I got older. It was big enough inside for just the two of us, a stool for my father and a little oil stove in winter. It used to get pretty cold though. Our stand was near a subway entrance, and at night when lots of people went home from work I'd stand out in front and bawl as loud as I could 'Evening papers! Get your evening papers here!' One night a big man in an overcoat stopped and asked me how old I was, and when I told him I was seven he said I'd have to go to school. So after that I went to public school every day. But on Saturdays and all summer, I used to help my father; and on Sunday afternoons we'd shut up shop and go to the park, or the zoo, or take a ride on a ferry boat. We had a pretty good time. But then a year ago my father took sick and died."

Jay and Mr. Freebody got up to put more logs in the kiln, but now the boy didn't seem to want to stop, and he went on talking to Garnet and her father. He was thin, too thin, and his ears stuck out like two pink shells with the firelight behind them.

"The landlady of the boardinghouse where we lived was real good to me; she told me I could stay on there for a while but I knew my father had a cousin named Nelson living in Oregon, he'd stayed with us once in Minnesota and my father'd always liked him. I thought

46

maybe I could go out there and stay with him and work on his farm, so I wrote him a letter. The landlady, Mrs. Cady her name was, wanted me to wait for an answer but I wanted to get out of the city as fast as I could when the newsstand was sold. Most of the money went to pay bills, and there wasn't much left. Mrs. Cady gave me enough for bus fare across the country.

"I didn't ride on the bus much though. I saved the money for food and hitchhiked. At night I slept in haystacks, and old barns, and once when it was raining I spent the night in an empty drainpipe beside the road. It took me three weeks to reach Oregon and when I got to Slaneyville where my cousin lived, they told me in the post office there that he had sold his farm and moved away a couple of months before. They didn't know where, nobody knew. I asked everyone who'd known him at all."

Garnet sat with her chin on her knees looking at Eric and listening. She was trying to imagine sleeping in a drainpipe with the rain making a noise on it, and the damp coming in at both ends. She was wondering what it would be like to be alone in the world as he was, with no mother or father or brothers; no roof, no bed, no food half the time, no comfort when you were afraid, no scoldings when you were bad. It was hard to imagine.

"Whatever did you do after that?" she asked.

"Well, it was summertime," said Eric. "A fellow there hired me to pick tomatoes for a cannery. While it was warm I could always get jobs picking stuff on the big farms. I made enough money to eat, and keep myself in shoes and overalls; then when I had a little bit extra I'd start hitchhiking again till it ran out, and then I'd get me another job. When people asked questions I

47

told them I was going home to my folks in New York. It was part true; I felt I'd be better off if I worked back towards the East, then if I got in a jam I could go back to Mrs. Cady and she'd help me out. But I didn't want to do it unless I had to. When they still asked questions I'd usually manage to skip out somewhere. I didn't want people interfering with me then, and I don't now." He frowned.

"Take it easy, boy," said Mr. Freebody who had sat down again. "Nobody ain't agoing to interfere with you. They got too much trouble of their own."

"Okay," said Eric apologetically. "Well, anyway, I guess I've picked just about everything there is: tomatoes in Oregon, and berries, and melons; sugar beets in the big fields in Utah and Colorado and later in the summer there were apples and pears and peaches in the orchards everywhere. In the fall I shucked corn in Kansas and Missouri. Some of the guys were swell to work for and some were mean as dirt and paid us next to nothing and were even stingy about the drinking water. I met all kinds of folks, all kinds of kids, some of them making their own livings the way I do. I got into fights and out of them and I made friends, and I had some good times and some rotten ones, and I didn't starve either, though sometimes, like tonight, I came close to it.

"In the winter it was harder. I stayed in the towns mostly and got jobs washing dishes in lunch wagons and eating places. When I broke a dish I had to pay for it, so I got pretty good after a while, but I don't ever want to see another fried egg as long as I live. Once I worked for a road gang hauling buckets of sand and water, and once I did odd jobs in a garage. I learned to drive when I was there, and I got so I knew a lot about a car.

"In Kansas City I got me a shoe box and shined shoes for ten cents a shine, but a cop there asked me a lot of questions and I got scared. Some of the kids I'd met that bum their way around like I do told me you could get long rides on freight trains if you were smart, so I got some chocolate and some oranges, sold my shoe box to a fellow, and went down to the train yards at night. There was a freight train on a siding and one of the boxcar doors was open. I crawled in and hid behind a crate. After a long time, a couple of hours I bet, someone shut the door and the train began moving. I never knew how long I was there because it was pitch black and I slept a lot. I had enough to eat but I got awful thirsty.

"Finally one night I woke up and wondered why it was so still. Then I knew the train had stopped. The door was open again and moonlight was coming in. I figured this was my chance to skip out; I thought we oughta be somewhere in the East by this time. Well I inched over to the door. Two men were talking on the platform outside; I thought they would never go away. One was telling the other about a toothache he'd had for a week. The other fellow said he oughta have the tooth pulled, but the first one said no, he'd rather keep the ache. Gee I thought they'd *never* go away. But they did after a while and I skinned out. I felt stiff all over like an old man, and when I thought I was safe enough to look around the first thing I saw was big mountains all shiny with snow in the moonlight. Where do you suppose I was?" Eric looked up and laughed. "In Colorado, that's where. All that way back again; I felt pretty dumb."

"What happened then?" asked Jay. His eyes were sparkling with excitement. Garnet could tell that he was envying this boy his life of independence and adventure. She didn't envy him, though, for anything but his courage and enterprise.

"I had a bad time after that," said Eric, frowning again. "I don't like to remember it or talk about it. But I got out all right; I always do!"

It was very late. The brilliant firelight and strong shadows gave the place a quality of strangeness. You felt that anything was possible in this moment.

"Look here," said Garnet's father suddenly. "You seem like a person with some sense. Maybe I could use you on my farm for a while. I'm building a new barn and though Jay's pretty good as a helper, I think that if I had two boys working instead of one, I'd get through a lot faster. Would you like to try it?"

Eric's face lit up. "I'd like it fine," he answered. "And I'd work like a steer, I swear I would."

"I'll pay you what I can," said Garnet's father, "and you'll have a place to live and food to eat."

"It'll be swell to have another boy around," said Jay.

Three brothers, thought Garnet? Would she like that? She believed she would but wasn't sure. All the same it was exciting to have a stranger come out of the woods that way and be adopted.

She felt tired now, and leaving the men and boys to talk among themsleves, stole back to her blanket under the chokecherry tree. The night sky spread black and huge above her, and the night sounds had diminished. It was the stillest hour in the world as though all things held their breath perilously, waiting for day to begin.

When she woke up there was heavy dew on everything. The first red rays of the sun touched the watery earth and made it glitter with a thousand rainbow colors. The kiln fire seemed pale and insignificant now, dimmed by the light of day. Near by Jay and Eric lay sound asleep, and her father and Mr. Freebody snatched a moment of rest under a tree. Mr. Freebody was snoring deeply and magnificently. Major was the only other person awake; he had discovered a new delicious smell and was following it anxiously across the grass, shaking his ears and snuffing.

"Major!" called Garnet under her breath, and the dog came wagging over to her and pushed his black, cold nose into her hand. His coat was soaked with dew.

She got up and put fresh coffee in the pot and climbed the narrow foot path to the top of the kiln again. On her way back she stopped and looked down at Eric curiously. She thought it might be nice to have him live with them for a while. His short upper lip and blunt tiptilted nose had a look of stubborn independence even in sleep; and she knew that his closed lids hid eyes that were clear and thoughtful. Yes, it was a nice face, but too thin. He was too thin all over; his collar bone stuck out like a coat hanger, and sharp wrists protruded from sleeves that were too short.

Her look wakened him; the eyelids flew open suddenly, and his face was alive again. His eyebrows twisted in bewilderment.

Garnet laughed. "I'm not dangerous," she explained. "Don't look so suspicious. I'm Garnet Linden and you're going to come home with us and live there as long as you want to. Remember?"

"Gee, for a minute I thought it was a dream," sighed Eric in relief.

Mr. Freebody woke himself up with an earth-shaking snore and started up guiltily.

"Almost fell asleep that time," he remarked.

Garnet looked at Eric and he looked at her. Their

51

mouths twitched and they choked on laughter they tried hard to swallow. They shared a private joke at someone's else expense; and suddenly they knew that they were friends.

At seven o'clock they heard the Hausers in their truck a mile away. Merle and Cicero raised healthy, tone-deaf voices and sang because they felt good.

"Neither of them fellas is ever going to make a crooner," said Mr. Freebody, as the singing came nearer and nearer, and got worse and worse.

Jay and Eric sat in the back seat on the way home, and Garnet in front with her father. The green fields fled by on either side. Far, far across the valley a pale streamer of smoke rose from thick woods to show where the kiln still burned. What a night it had been! I will never forget it, Garnet told herself.

The Ford toiled up the slope to their house, lurched in at the gate and shuddered to a stop.

Garnet's mother came out to meet her sooty family. She looked fresh and rosy; and Donald at her side was still spotlessly clean because he had only been up for ten minutes.

Garnet's mother laughed.

"You look like charcoal burners and chimney sweeps," she cried. Then she noticed Eric. "Who is this?"

Garnet pushed Eric forward. He had shoulder blades like a pair of wings.

"This is someone new to belong to our family," she said. "His name is Eric, and he appeared at midnight."

Mrs. Linden was the mother of three children and hardly anything surprised her any more.

"Come in," she said. "There are griddlecakes for breakfast. While you're eating them I'll find out all about you."

Garnet went to wash her face and hands.

"I have a nice mother," she thought to herself. "I have a nice family."

It made her feel safe and warm to know that she belonged to them and they to her. No she didn't envy Eric. Not one bit.

In the dim mirror above the sink her face surprised her. It was dark with soot and there were four black stripes along her cheek where she had laid her fingers.

The air was beautiful with the smell of griddlecakes. Garnet splashed, splashed the water over her face and neck and scrubbed and scrubbed with the soap. Blindly she reached for the towel. She could hardly wait to get back to her family; and to the griddlecakes.

V. Locked In

A S THE days went by it seemed as if there was nothing that Eric couldn't do. He was handy with hammer and saw; he could milk a cow and drive a team or a
tractor, he knew all about gardens, and separators, and
harness, and often he could tell what the weather would
be like the next day. He helped old Henry Jones chisel
limestone slabs for the strong piers that were to be the
foundation of the barn; and besides all these things he
could walk on his hands and do flip-ups, swim like a fish
and dive seven different ways; he could talk about far-
away places, and people he'd seen and adventures he'd
had; and he could eat even more than Jay. He was
wonderful.

They all liked him; but after a while Garnet began to

feel a little lonely. Jay always wanted to be with Eric and never with her any more. The boys worked together all day, and in the evenings went down to the river for a swim, or to the bridge to fish. When Garnet wanted to go along Jay was apt to discourage her by saying, "You'd better not come. Eric and I have to talk."

She played often with Citronella nowadays. Eric helped them to build a house in the branches of a big oak tree in the pasture. He made a little ladder for them to climb up to the first branch which was about six feet from the ground. Halfway up the tree they built a sort of platform with a railing, and on the spreading boughs above laid laths and dead branches for a roof. It was just big enough for the two girls, and often they spent hours there, the wind swaying them a little and the starlings chattering and whistling in the leaves above. It was great fun while it was new, but by the time they had finished it, and hauled up an old chair at the risk of breaking their necks, and eaten their lunch there every day for a week, the newness had worn off.

One grey afternoon in early August they were sitting there, and Garnet searching in her mind for something new to do, said, "Let's tell stories. You tell the first one, Citronella, because I thought of it."

It had been one of those dull, dull days when nothing interesting happens and everything goes wrong. It was the kind of day that you stub your toe a lot and lose things, and forget what it was that your mother asked you to get at the store. Garnet kept swallowing great, hollow yawns and wishing that something would happen: an earthquake, or an escaped hyena from a circus. Anything!

"Come on, Citronella, tell a story," she commanded,

and lay down on the floor with her legs propped comfortably against the tree trunk.

Citronella sighed and began. "Well," she said, "once upon a time there was a beautiful young lady sixteen years old. Her name was Mabel and she was very rich. She was so rich that she had a cellar full of gold pieces. She lived all alone in a big brick house on the top of a hill; at least she had a hired girl and a hired man but she didn't have any folks, I mean."

"Where were they" asked Garnet.

"Dead," replied Citronella. "Well, and besides the gold pieces, she had hundreds of necklaces and bracelets made of emeralds and diamonds and sapphires, and she wore white satin dresses for every day. And she had a little automobile just big enough for her and nobody else. And she had a dog that could talk."

"Go on!" jeered Garnet. "I never heard of a dog that could talk."

"This one could. It was a French poodle and it talked French."

"What's a French poodle?" inquired Garnet suspiciously.

"Oh, a kind of a dog from France," answered Citronella with a vague wave of her hand. "Quit interrupting or I can't go on. Well, and Mabel had a swimming pool, too, and a little gold piano, and guess what else she had! She had a room with a soda fountain in it. It had all different kinds of faucets on it: a strawberry faucet, and a vanilla one, and chocolate and pineapple and maple. It makes me hungry to tell about it."

"Me too," agreed Garnet. "Well go on, what happened to her?"

"One day she went out riding in her little automobile.

She drove and drove for a long time on a deserted road with trees on either side. It was beginning to get dark and she was just going to turn around and start home when she saw a poor old ragged man beside the road. He looked very sad and awful tired and there were burrs in his beard. She stopped the car and said, 'Old man, what's the matter?' And he said, 'I've come a long way and I'm hungry. I want something to eat.' So Mabel said, 'Well jump in my car and I'll take you to my house,' and he did."

"But you said the car was just big enough for one," objected Garnet.

"Well, all right, he rode on the running board then. And when they got to her house she took him to the soda fountain and made him a maple-nut sundae, and a chocolate fudge sundae, and a strawberry ice-cream soda. He felt much better after that and he said, 'Look at me, Mabel.' And she looked at him, and suddenly he changed into a real handsome young man. 'Gee!' Mabel said. And he told her he was a rich prince and a witch had changed him into an old man and said he'd have to stay like that till someone did him a good deed. So then he asked Mabel to marry him and she said she would, and they lived happy ever after."

"And then what?" asked Garnet.

"That's all, " said Citronella, "they lived happy ever after."

Garnet sighed. "You always tell stories about people that are grown up and fall in love. I like stories about children and wild animals and explorers." She sat up suddenly. "I know what. Let's go to town to the library and read. It's still early and it's going to rain anyway."

Citronella objected for a minute or two because she

said she didn't feel like walking all that way just to read a book. But Garnet was sure they could get a ride with someone and soon persuaded her to come.

As luck would have it the moment they went out of the gate they saw Mr. Freebody's truck clattering down the road towards them. They waved and called and Mr. Freebody stopped and opened the door to let them in. He was going to town to buy feed.

"We'd rather ride outside, if you don't mind," said Garnet, and the two girls scrambled into the back of the truck and stood up holding onto the roof over the driver's seat.

It was fun to ride like that because as soon as he got on the highway Mr. Freebody drove very fast and the wind blew so hard against them that Garnet's pigtails stuck straight out behind, and Citronella's bang stood up on end like a hedge. They felt as though their noses were blown flat against their faces, and when they spoke their words flew away from them.

"I feel like a thing on the front of a boat," shouted Garnet. "A figurehead, I think it's called."

Citronella had never heard of figureheads and it was hard to explain because you had to yell so; the wind roared and Mr. Freebody's truck was a very loud one. Also if you opened your mouth too wide lazy beetles on the wing were apt to be swept into it.

They watched the truck swallow up the flat ribbon of road like a tape-measure; the little grey town of Blaiseville flew towards them. There it was, all just as usual: the courthouse with its tower and gilded dome, the gasoline station, and the red painted depot, and Mrs. Elson's yellow house with clothes leaping on the line; unusually big clothes they were as Mrs. Elson and her husband were both immensely fat. There was Opal Clyde, the doctor's daughter, bouncing a ball on the walk in front of her house, and there was Junior Gertz pulling his dog along in a little express wagon. Garnet and Citronella waved as they rode grandly by. Mr. Freebody drew up in front of the Farm Bureau; the truck coughed hoarsely once or twice and subsided into stillness. The girls jumped down.

"How you two little girls going to git home?" asked Mr. Freebody.

"Oh, we'll walk maybe," answered Garnet. "Or get a ride with someone," added Citronella hopefully.

They thanked him and walked up the Main Street past the blacksmith's and the drugstore and the post office. There was a bulletin in the post-office window that said: "Big Hollow Ladies Annual Picnic Next Sunday. Come One, Come All!" Garnet giggled at this notice, seeing in her mind a group of huge balloon-like creatures in dresses eating sandwiches under a tree. Of course she knew that the Big Hollow Ladies were simply ladies that lived in Big Hollow, but it had a funny sound all the same. They went on up the street past the store full of straw hats and overalls, and the shoe store, and the "Sweet Eat Shop" where the mechanical piano was making a noise like an old hurdy-gurdy in a boiler factory.

Finally on the outskirts of the town they came to the library, an old-fashioned frame building set back from the road among thick-foliaged maple trees.

Garnet loved the library; it smelled deliciously of old books and was full of stories that she had never read. Miss Pentland, the librarian, was a nice little fat lady who sat behind an enormous desk facing the door.

"Good afternoon, Citronella," she said, smiling. "Good afternoon, Ruby."

Miss Pentland always called Garnet Ruby by mistake. There were so many little girls in Blaiseville with names like jewels that it was very confusing. There were Ruby Schwarz, Ruby Harvey, and Rubye Smalley, Pearl Orison and Pearl Schoenbecker, Beryl Schultz, and little Opal Clyde.

Garnet and Citronella poked about among the books until each had found the one she wanted and then they settled down on a broad window seat between two tall cases of large old volumes that looked as if they hadn't been opened by anyone for fifty years.

Garnet had *The Jungle Book*, and Citronella with a sigh of pleasure began to read a wonderful story called *Duchess Olga; or the Sapphire Signet*.

Many times the screen door of the library creaked and closed with a muffled bang as people came and went; other children and grown people, old ladies looking for books on crocheting and boys wanting stories about G-men. For a while rain splintered against the window beside the two girls but they scarcely heard it. Garnet was thousands of miles away with Kotick, the white seal, swimming the wide seas to find a safe island for his people; and Citronella was in a ballroom lighted by a hundred chandeliers and crowded with beautiful ladies and gentlemen in full evening dress.

Garnet finished "The White Seal" and went on to "Toomai of the Elephants." Once she looked up and stretched. "My, it's quiet," she whispered. "I wonder if it's late."

"Oh, we haven't been here long," said Citronella impatiently. She had reached the most exciting part of the book where Duchess Olga was being lowered on a rope down the face of a huge cliff. The trouble was that the man who held the rope didn't like Duchess Olga and was planning to let her drop at any minute. Citronella thought everything would turn out all right in the end but she wasn't sure.

By the time that Garnet had re-read "Rikki-Tikki-Tavi," and Duchess Olga had been rescued pages back and safely returned to the ballroom, the light began to fade.

"What does the word 'insidious' mean?" asked Citronella, but Garnet didn't know.

"My, it is kind of still here," she went on. "I'll ask Miss Pentland what time it is." She disappeared behind the bookcases.

"Garnet!" she called loudly the next moment. "Miss Pentland's gone! Everyone's gone!"

Garnet leaped from the window seat. It was true; there was no one there. They ran to the door, but it was firmly locked. The back door was locked too; and the heavy glass windows had not been opened in years; they stuck in their frames as if set in cement. It was impossible to move them.

"Good night!" moaned Citronella. "We're locked in!" She was on the verge of tears.

But Garnet felt pleasantly excited.

"Citronella," she said solemnly, "this is an adventure. Things like this happen to people in books; we'll be able to tell our children and grandchildren about it. I hope we stay here all night!"

"Oh gee," sobbed Citronella. She wished with all her heart that she hadn't read *Duchess Olga*; it was too scary. She simply had no courage left. If only she had picked out a good peaceful book about boarding school girls or something, she wouldn't be so frightened now.

Suddenly she had such a terrible thought that she stopped crying.

"Garnet!" she cried. "Do you know what day it is? Saturday! That means we'll be here till day after tomorrow. We'll starve!"

Garnet's excitement went flat. It would be awful to stay in here as long as that.

"Let's bang on the windows," she suggested. "Maybe someone will come."

They banged on the glass and shouted at the tops of their lungs. But the library was some distance from the street, and the thick maples deadened the noise they made. Blaiseville people were peacefully eating their suppers and never heard a sound.

Slowly the dusk sifted into the room. The bookcases looked tall and solemn, and the pictures on the wall were solemn too: steel engravings of Napoleon at Elba, and Washington Crossing the Delaware.

There was no telephone in the library and no electric light. There were gas fixtures but Garnet and Citronella could not find any matches. They rummaged through Miss Pentland's desk but it was full of useless things like filing cards, rubber stamps, elastic bands and neat little rolls of string.

Citronella pounced upon a chocolate bar in a pigeonhole.

"We won't starve right away anyhow," she said, brightening a little. "I don't think Miss Pentland would mind if we ate it, do you?"

"We'll buy her another when we get out," said Garnet; so they divided it and stood, sadly munching, at the window nearest the street.

The twilight deepened.

"Who is that!" cried Garnet suddenly. They saw a dim, small figure slowly approaching on the cement walk that led to the library door. The person seemed to be bowing.

Citronella began thumping on the window joyously. "It's Opal Clyde, bouncing her ball," she said. "Yell, Garnet. Yell and bang."

They both yelled and banged; and Opal after a scared glance at the dark window scurried down the path as fast as she could go, without coming nearer to see what was making the noise.

"Do you think she'll tell someone?" asked Citronella anxiously.

"Oh, she thought it was a spook," said Garnet in disgust. "Probably no one will believe her if she does."

They watched hopefully. All over Blaiseville the street lamps blossomed suddenly with light, but only a faint gleam penetrated the maple leaves. The two girls heard cars coming and going and faint shouts of children playing in back yards. They pounded and called till they were hoarse and their knuckles ached. But nobody came.

After a while they gave it up as a bad job and returned to the window seat.

The room was very dark now; strange, unknown and filled with shadows. It was as though it wakened at nightfall; as though it breathed and wakened and began to wait. There were tiny creaking sounds and rustlings, and airy scamperings of mouse feet.

"I don't like it," whispered Citronella. "I don't like it all: My own voice scares me. I don't dare talk out loud."

"Neither do I," murmured Garnet. "I feel as if all those books were alive and listening."

"I wonder why our folks don't come after us," said Citronella.

"They don't know where we are, that's why!" answered Garnet. "They don't even know we came to town: and we didn't tell Mr. Freebody that we were going to the library."

"I wish I'd never learned to read," sighed Citronella. "I wish I was some kind of animal and didn't have to be educated."

"It might be fun to be a panther," agreed Garnet, "or a kangaroo, or a monkey."

"Or a pig, even," said Citronella. "A safe, happy pig asleep in its own pen with its own family!"

"One that had never seen a library and couldn't even spell pork," added Garnet, and giggled. Citronella giggled too, and they both felt much better.

Outside the night wind stirred among the trees, and a maple scratched at the window glass with a thin finger; but inside it was close and still except for the small mysterious sounds that can be heard in all old houses after dark.

Garnet and Citronella huddled together and whispered. They heard the court-house clock strike eight, then nine; but when it struck ten they were both sound asleep.

At a little before midnight they were wakened by a tremendous pounding and shouting.

"Who? What's that? Where am I?" shrieked Citronella in a panic, and Garnet, her heart thumping, said, "In the library, remember? Someone's at the door."

She ran forward in the dark, barking her shins and whacking her elbows on unfamiliar surfaces.

"Who's there?" she called.

"That you, Garnet? Thank the Lord we've found you at last," said a voice that was unmistakably Mr. Freebody's. "Is Citronella with you? Fine! Both your dads are scouring the town for you. Open the door!"

"But we're locked *in*, Mr. Freebody," called Garnet. "Miss Pentland has the key."

"I'll get it. I'll get it," shouted Mr. Freebody excitedly. "You wait there."

"We can't do anything *but* wait," said Citronella crossly. She was always cross when she first woke up.

In a little while they heard rapid footsteps on the front walk, and voices, and then the lovely sound of a key turning in the lock. Miss Pentland, with her hat on sideways, rushed in and embraced them.

"You poor little things!" she cried. "Such a thing has *never* happened before; I always make sure everyone's gone before I lock up. I can't understand how I missed you!"

"That's all right, Miss Pentland," said Garnet. "It was an adventure. And we ate your chocolate!"

Garnet's father and Mr. Freebody and Mr. Hauser came in too, all talking and exclaiming.

"Are you both sure you're all right?" asked Mr. Hauser anxiously, his fat, kind face looking pale for the first time in years.

"We're all right, Papa," said Citronella. "But we're awfully hungry."

"I'll go telephone the folks at home," volunteered Mr. Freebody. "So's they won't have to worry no longer. You better take the little girls down to the lunch wagon for a bite. Only place that's open at this hour."

The lunch wagon was down by the railroad tracks; neither Garnet nor Citronella had ever been there before. It was full of bright yellow light, and cigar smoke, and powerful food smells. It was wonderful to go there so late at night and eat fried egg sandwiches and apple pie and tell everybody what had happened to them.

"Yes sir!" said Mr. Freebody coming in the door. "Don't you be fooled! Those ain't two little girls you see settin' up there; those are two genuwine bookworms, couldn't stop reading long enough to come home. Planning to take up permanent residence in the liberry from now on, ain'tcha?"

Everyone laughed.

"Just the same," whispered Garnet to Citronella. "I sort of wish they hadn't found us until morning. Then we could have told our grandchildren that once we stayed in the public library all night long!"

VI. Journey

THE LONG days of August were filled with acti-
vity. The barn took shape rapidly and it was going
to be a fine one. Every now and then Mr. Freebody
would pause before it and shake his head.

"My, that sure is a pretty barn," he would say dreamily. "That sure is pretty as a peach."

The warm air rang with the sound of saw and hammer.
While the men worked on the barn Garnet and her
mother had their hands full with the house and garden;
for now the garden was yielding in all its abundance. It
was hard to keep up with it. When you had finished
picking all the beans it was time to pick the yellow
squashes, shaped like hunting horns. And when you got
through with the squash it was time for the beans again.
And then you had to hurry, hurry and gather the
bursting ripe tomatoes from the heavy vines, for canning. Then there were beets and carrots to be attended
to, and after that it was time for the beans again.

"Beans never know when to stop!" said Garnet's
mother in annoyance.

Corn was picked every day; and that was pleasant,
walking in the rustling good-smelling aisles between the

stalks. And the watermelons! Big solid green ones that Garnet thumped with a finger to see if they sounded ripe. And every now and then she dropped one on purpose and it would burst open, cold as a glacier and rosy red. Then she would walk homeward dripping and drooling, spitting out black seeds and feeling fine.

And canning! Oh those weeks of harvesting and peeling and preparing apples, peaches, tomatoes, cucumbers, plums and beans. All day the kitchen smelled like heaven and was filled with steam. The stove was covered with kettles and vats, and upside down on the window-sill stood processions of mason jars full of bright color and hot to the touch.

Then in the middle of it all came the time for threshing.

Several weeks before, Mr. Linden had mowed his oat fields, and Garnet had helped Jay and Eric stack the tied yellow bundles in shocks: six yellow bundles with their heads bowed together and a seventh on top, like a hat. When they were finished the field was dotted with oat shocks like other fields all up and down the valley; it looked nice. But now the oats were dry, and ready for threshing.

Every year Mr. Linden rented the Hausers' threshing machine for one day. That meant that Mr. Hauser and Cicero and Merle came with it and helped. Mr. Freebody was always on hand and Jasper Cardiff and his two sons always came down from Big Hollow. Some of the men would bring their wives with them to visit and help Mrs. Linden with the cooking; threshers eat a lot. Already there were cakes in the pantry, and five different kinds of pie nestled under clean dish towels. There were new loaves of bread too, and at dinner time there would be pork and beans, and mountains of mashed potato, and oceans of gravy. The big agate coffeepot would be simmering on the stove, and by half past twelve every single thing would be gone! Garnet remembered other threshings.

Early in the morning she heard the grumble of a tractor and the toot of a whistle on a threshing machine and looked out of the window to see the pair of them lumbering across the fields toward the new barn. The thresher had a long neck like a dinosaur, with a sort of fringed mustache on the end of it to keep the oat straw from blowing too far. It was a huge gangling machine covered with wheels and belts and pipes and bolts; it looked almost too complicated to be efficient.

By the time Garnet finished her housework and got outdoors, the threshing was well under way.

Mr. Hauser sat like an emperor upon the seat of the tractor which was attached to the threshing machine by a long swiftly sliding belt. Men tossed bundles of oats onto a moving ramp which fed them into the wildly gnashing jaws of the thresher. Inside of the monster some mysterious process went on which separated the kernels from the stalks. The kernels were swept in gusts down a long pipe at one side; it had two mouths on which Cicero Hauser was tenderly fastening burlap bags which filled as rapidly as he could replace them. Straw and chaff flew out of the pipe that looked like a dinosaur's neck, and clouds of golden dust filled the air. Men worked hard, pitching the bundles, packing down the straw, and hauling heavy oat sacks to the little granary by the new barn. Mr. Freebody sat high on the front of the machine, steering its long neck with a wheel, helping to build the strawstack tall, firm, and symmetrical.

"What can I do, Daddy?" Garnet asked her father, and sneezed. The flying chaff tickled and choked her and got into her eyes. She felt itchy all over, but it was fun; everyone was working together in such speed and excitement. She wanted to have a part in it.

"Well — " said her father, considering, "you might help Cicero with the oat sacks; or you can throw on bundles that have fallen on the ground. There're lots of things you could do."

Cicero showed her how to wrap the burlap sacks around the pipe mouths and hold them tight with a metal clamp; and how, when one sack was full, to push a lever towards the other one, so that the oats would fall into that. You had to work fast or oats spilled on the ground and were wasted. Above the roar of the motor it was nice to hear the smooth swift rush of kernels down the pipe.

When she had worked there for nearly an hour Garnet helped toss bundles onto the moving ramp. Jay worked beside her, pitching and perspiring and grunting with fatigue. He looked serious and important, and when she spoke to him he answered shortly.

By and by Garnet climbed up on top of the machine to see what Mr. Freebody was doing. His eyebrows and big mustache were full of chaff, and he looked like an old walrus that had got mixed up with some seaweed.

"I could eat an elephant," he told Garnet, "a nice roasted elephant, with onions and brown gravy. In fact I think an elephant's the only thing that would be enough of a meal to satisfy me right now."

Garnet laughed. "We aren't having it though," she said. "Our butcher doesn't carry it. But we *have* got five different kinds of pie: apple, peach, blueberry, lemon, and butterscotch!"

Mr. Freebody closed his eyes for a minute and sighed as if this was too much for him.

"Next to roast elephant I like pie best of all," he said.

Ahead of them the glittering stack grew slowly taller till it was like a little mountain made of spun gold. Eric moved about on top of it, packing it down and making it even with a pitchfork. Every now and then he lost his balance and fell into the soft straw; Garnet and Mr. Freebody laughed loudly and rudely every time this happened.

"Wait here a minute," said Mr. Freebody suddenly. "Them boys ain't getting the loads in quick enough. I better go help 'em pitch. You take this over, Garnet. I'll show you how to work it." And he explained to her that the wheel on the left turned the great pipe from side to side, and the wheel on right raised it up and down.

"Do you think it'll be all right?" asked Garnet nervously.

"Oh it's gentle as a baby," said Mr. Freebody. " 'T would eat right out of your hand if you'd let it. Just pat its neck once in a while and handle the wheels like I said, and it'll go on blowing its durndest till the cows come home."

All the same Garnet felt extremely important as she turned the pipe slowly to what she considered a good position and pulled the rope which lifted its long mustache, and allowed the straw to blow all the way back over the stack. The golden smoke of chaff and straw thickened the air, and her arms and legs were covered with a shining dust.

Eric climbed down from the pile to get a drink of water; the engine roared and chugged, and the sun of noonday burned in all its glory. Garnet felt drowsy; she sat up straight, opened her eyes very wide, tried humming a song, but it didn't do any good. Pretty soon her head dropped anyway, and her thoughts began turning slowly, strangely, into dreams.

"Look out!" shouted a loud voice behind her, and she lifted her head. Then she grabbed the wheel and held onto it in bewilderment. Could it be an earthquake? Was she dizzy? Because now the golden mountain had begun to move by itself. It was moving toward her, and towering above her, and suddenly beginning to slip slowly and then faster over and upon her, till she was engulfed, half smothered by dry, tickling, prickling yellow straw. She understood then that the pile must have become top-heavy and capsized.

Eric came to her rescue, dug her out and brushed the clinging straw from her clothes.

"That was stupid of me," said Garnet. She felt awful.

"Oh think nothing of it," said Eric. "I should've been on the job instead of getting a drink. We'll have it all piled up again in a jiffy anyway."

But Jay came towards her scowling.

"Well for Pete's sake!" he said angrily. "You certainly made a mess of it that time all right! Why don't you stay home and help mother? Threshing isn't anything for girls to be monkeying with anyway; home with a dish towel, that's where you belong! This will slow up the whole works."

Garnet turned and ran across the hot fields. The oat stubble stood up like little lances and hurt her bare feet, and grasshoppers popped and scattered like sparks from a fire. Tears filled her eyes and made the meadow surge and swim before her in a golden flood.

"Hateful Jay! Mean, mean, mean," she cried under her breath; "I won't ever feel the same about him again. I hate him."

Oh Jay, what has happened to you, she thought. Jay who had been her best friend always, and who had considered her his equal in many things — well practically his equal anyway. Ever since Eric had come he had been different. And now just think how he had spoken to her! As if she were a baby, or a sissy, or somebody he didn't like.

She turned back towards the house and went up the path through the garden. Maybe her mother would make her feel all right again.

The kitchen seemed to be filled with women. Mrs. Hauser and her sister were sitting fat and solid on a bench, and old Mrs. Eberhardt rocked and creaked in the rocking chair. Two Cardiff ladies were busy at the sink and about their feet Donald and a little Cardiff crawled and shouted. Mrs. Linden was opening the oven door and laughing at something someone had said. The air rang with women's voices and the shouting of small children. Clearly this was no time to disturb her mother, and Garnet, unnoticed, stole up the stairway to her little room. It would be hot up there under the eaves, but it would be quiet at least and nobody would bother her. She pushed open the half closed door and stopped.

There on her bed, fat, pleased with himself, and babbling, lay the youngest Hauser baby, Leroy. He was red and dimpled and fair-haired and Garnet had always liked him until today. But now she looked at him coldly as he waved his legs and arms, and showed his two teeth in a foolish smile, and she felt that she positively loathed him.

"All right!" said Garnet severely to the baby. "There's

no room for me in my own house, and they don't want me out at the threshing, and I'll just go away, that's all. Just go away by myself!"

She washed, combed her hair, and put on a blue dress and a pair of strapped shoes. The shoes felt stiff and uncomfortable to toes that had gone bare all summer, and there was starch in the collar of the dress that scratched her neck. She hated dresses anyway, and buttoning the difficult small buttons she hiccuped with sobs. No one has ever been so unhappy before, she thought to herself. Maybe they'll all be sorry later on!

In the shiny pocketbook that her grandmother had sent her for Christmas there was half a dollar, a new handkerchief, the silver thimble that she had found weeks ago, and a bottle of perfume from the dime store. She wound the link chain tight around her wrist and wondered whether or not to wear her hat. She took it out of the closet and looked at it. It was a yellow hat made of cheap straw and it poked up on top of the crown. Garnet thought it was the sort of hat that the pig in the nursery rhyme might have worn to market. When she put it on and looked in the mirror at her red nose and long sad pigtails under the dejected hat brim, she pulled it off in a fury and threw it on the floor. Leroy blew a big bubble in appreciation.

"Oh you!" grumbled Garnet. "Why don't you stay home in your own crib!"

She creaked down the stairs in her uncomfortable shoes and slipped through the kitchen.

"Where are you going Garnet?" called her mother above the fat voices of the women. "Dinner's almost ready."

"Oh, just out," replied Garnet vaguely. "I'm not

76

hungry anyway. Too many people around." She closed the screen door behind her; she didn't care if she *was* rude. No one suspected the hot little fire of anger and despair that burned beneath her ribs.

She began to run now, sliding in her slippery shoes. She didn't want anyone to stop her, and she saw Mr. Freebody ambling across the field.

"Hey there!" shouted Mr. Freebody, but Garnet pretended not to hear him and ran all the faster.

When she had reached the highway her anger began to turn into a feeling of excitement. She hadn't planned where she would go, but Eric's stories of hitchhiking were still fresh in her mind. I'll try it anyway, she thought, and stopped at the roadside; he isn't the only one who can travel and do things by himself!

The first car that passed was full of people, and as the second approached she held up her hand. The car slowed down, and to her horror she saw that she knew the people inside: Miss Pentland, her old mother, and two smiley ladies from Big Hollow.

"It's little Ruby Linden," Garnet heard Miss Pentland shouting to her mother who was deaf. "Good morning, Ruby! Did you want to drive into Blaiseville?"

Garnet wanted nothing less. She was in a bad temper, and her feelings were hurt, and she wanted to be far away from all the people and objects that she knew. And anyhow, what adventure was to be had in a closed coupe, being polite to these four nice ladies.

"Why no — no thank you," stammered Garnet, "I just waved, that's all."

"All right, dear," said Miss Pentland. "Hot, isn't it?"

It was hot. Heat trembled over the shining road. Garnet watched it anxiously.

A fat little roadster rounded the bend and she again raised her hand; but this time the car whistled by her without even slowing down. She felt rebuffed.

Two more cars and a truck passed in the same manner; but finally an old black sedan wobbled to a stop beside her. "Want a lift?" asked the man at the wheel, and his wife smiled encouragingly, a brilliant smile with a gold tooth in it.

"Yes, please, I do," said Garnet gratefully, feeling like an explorer embarking on a perilous journey.

"How far are you aiming to go, little girl?" asked the woman.

For a second Garnet wondered frantically what to tell her. Then she decided.

"New Conniston," she answered firmly. New Conniston was eighteen miles away. To Garnet who had never seen a larger city it seemed enormous and as glamorous as Bagdad, or Zanzibar, or Constantinople. It was a town built on a steep hill. There were trolley cars there, department stores, and three different kinds of dime stores. There was a movie theatre, and a little park with a fountain in it and some old Civil War cannons. Garnet had been there only three or four times in her life, and never by herself.

"New Conniston!" said the lady. "Well, we ain't going quite so far as that; only to Hodgeville. But maybe you can get the bus from there."

Garnet sat in the middle of the backseat by herself, and looked at the backs of their necks. The man's was thin and wiry and brown with sun and crisscrossed with lines. It looked all dried out like a piece of bark; a regular farmer's neck. But the woman's was fat and comfortable looking and she wore a bead necklace with a rhinestone clasp at the back. Her hat was just like anybody's hat.

The woman turned her full pink face towards Garnet and stared at her curiously.

"Seems to me like you're pretty young to be hitch-hiking," she remarked. "If I was your mama, I don't think I'd like it much."

Garnet's toes wriggled uncomfortably in her shoes. She didn't know what to say.

"Well, young folks are real enterprising nowadays," said the man. "Always was, I guess, and always will be. Why I remember when I was a kid once, I walked four-teen miles to see a circus. Just walked off and left my chores; left cows that needed milking and hogs that had to be fed, and I didn't say nothing to my folks be-cause I had a pretty good idea of what they'd think about it. I can remember right this minute how that circus tent looked, all lighted up like a birthday cake. I just had enough money to get me inside, and not a cent left over for pop or peanuts; and going off that way without supper, my stomach felt as empty as a rag-picker's pocket. Didn't care though. I saw the circus all through, elephants, lady horse-riders in tights and all the rest of it. Time I got home it was almost day-break, and my dad was waiting up. He took a strap to me, and I deserved it. But I always kind of felt it was worth it too."

Garnet thought probably it had been, but she didn't say so.

"Worth it nothing!" cried the woman indignantly. "Why your mother must've been half crazy with worry!"

Garnet decided to change the subject. She felt quite sure that this lady wouldn't approve of her own be-havior if she knew about it.

79

"Are you — do you live in Hodgeville?" she asked.

"No indeed," said the lady. "We live over to Deepwater, but we get up to Hodgeville pretty often."

"She's a singer," explained the man, jerking his head sideways at his wife. "Got one of the finest contralto voices you ever listened to. When she lets go of it full blast even the cookstove trembles. She sings at church festivals, and meetings all up and down the county. And besides that she takes in washing, and keeps house, and does fancy needlework. Won two ribbons at the fair last year, she did."

Garnet could tell that he was very proud of his wife. And she saw that the woman's cheeks had a rounder curve because she was beaming with pleasure.

"Oh I wish I could hear you sing once," said Garnet. "I never in my life heard a contralto!"

"Go on, sing something for the little girl, Ella," urged the man. "Let it rip. There's no one on the road."

"Well, let's see," said the woman patting her bead necklace and clearing her throat. "How about a hymn?"

"Yes!" cried Garnet. " 'Rock of Ages,' please." It was the only hymn she could remember.

Suddenly the woman began to sing. Garnet held onto the edge of the seat. "Rock of Ages, *cleft* for me," sang the woman; and Garnet understood about the cookstove trembling. She had never heard a voice so powerful before. It filled the sedan till her head reeled and her ears rang. And it floated richly and enormously out into the summer day. Garnet saw three little towheaded children on a fence with their mouths and eyes wide open in surprise; she saw a farmer put down his pitchfork and stare after them; she saw some cows in a pasture raise their heads in worry and bewilderment. And she felt as though in another minute the tremendous voice would blow her out of the window.

The song ended, and the woman turned her head expectantly.

"Well, how was that?" enquired the husband.

"Oh it was wonderful," said Garnet rather weakly. "I never heard anything so — so *huge* in all my life!"

"That's right," agreed the man. "If we could just hitch up the power in her voice, we could make enough electricity to light up the whole of New Conniston, I bet."

The first Hodgeville houses appeared. The woman settled her hat and looked at Garnet.

"You going to be all right now, dear?" she asked. "I'd take the bus from here if I was you. You never know what people you'll meet up with hitchhiking. Have you money enough?"

"Oh yes, I have quite a lot," replied Garnet thinking of her fine round half dollar still unspent. Why you could do a hundred different things with so much money. Ride on buses, eat enough ice cream to be uncomfortable, buy things in dime stores, maybe go to a movie even! Perhaps there would be a Western picture at the Dreamland Theater in New Conniston; she hoped so; one with plenty of horses and bloodshed.

The man stopped the car in the main street by the bus station.

"You're just in time, little girl," said he. "Bus going out of here in a couple of minutes."

"Don't get lost now," said the woman.

"You going to the fair to New Conniston when it comes?" asked her husband. "You look in the needlework section if you do; the quilts with the most prizes will be hers. Maybe we'll see you there. Zangl is the name."

"Mr. and Mrs. Earl Zangl," added his wife.

"I hope I will see you again," said Garnet. "Thank you for the ride and for the song."

They were nice people; for a minute she felt sorry to see them go. But in the next minute, she forgot about them and climbed into the bus.

VII. "As a Ragpicker's Pocket"

IT WAS an old bus but still jaunty looking, and the driver had a rose stuck in his cap, and a pencil behind one ear. He looked younger than the bus.

There were only two other people inside: a woman fanning herself with a newspaper, and a man asleep with his mouth open.

Garnet settled herself on a large slippery seat with a leatherette cover. The leatherettte had a rich, strong smell, and there were other smells besides, of gasoline and dust and people's clothes.

For a long time she watched flying farms and cornfields, woods and hills, the light was very bright. Dogs lay in the shade under trees, but cats slept on front doorsteps with the sun on their fur.

The bus stopped at Melody, the next town, and the man and woman got out, the man still yawning and rubbing his face, and the woman sighing and shaking her head about the heat. Nobody else got on. The driver turned and looked at Garnet.

"Like to go fast?" he asked. "The old bus has some speed in her still. I tell you what. You've got it all to yourself now; and you can pretend like you're a lady with a shofer. I'll show you some driving. How'll that be?"

"Oh I'd love it!" cried Garnet, and off they went.

They drove like fire, up hills and down; around curves on two wheels; and the telegraph poles rushed by like tall giraffes in a hurry. Birds flew from fences; hens rocketed out of the way, and the wind whistled.

Garnet bounced from side to side of the slippery seat and kept herself from squealing. This was better than the whip cars at the fair!

In no time at all they were in sight of the tall hill that was covered with the city of New Conniston. There it was, glittering for Garnet like Bagdad and Zanzibar and Constantinople. She shook her purse; there was still forty cents inside of it that jingled with promise.

They drove past the first shabby houses of the town, and then the larger ones, and then the stores, and then they stopped.

"Thank you for going so fast," said Garnet to the bus driver.

"Okay, sister," said he, helping her down. "I'm telling you it was a pleasure."

What shall I do first, she thought to herself. First I will just walk up and down the street and listen to the noise.

There was a lot of noise. Trolley cars clanged and clattered on the tracks, automobiles hooted, hundreds of people talked and talked, and their footsteps clicked and shuffled on the pavement all day long. Garnet liked to listen to the noise of a city, the noise of things happening.

Each time she came to a store she stopped and looked in the windows. There were a thousand different things in them that you never saw in Blaiseville. One big window was full of kitchen articles: a pale green stove, and a green porcelain sink; and enamel pots and pans all pale green. Who ever heard of such a thing! And there was a window full of evening gowns; and one with nothing but fur coats. Imagine. Now, in August, fur coats!

In each window Garnet selected a present for her family. The green sink for her mother, and a brown fur coat, and an evening gown like icicles. In Merchant-Farmer's big display window there was a discing machine that her father would like; and in a toy shop she saw a little fire chief's car just the right size for Donald to ride in.

But for Jay? For Jay — was she really thinking of a present for him? Why she hated him, didn't she? Hadn't she come all this long journey just because she hated him? Oh no! After all, no matter how she tried, Garnet couldn't even remember, now, how it felt to be angry with Jay. And just then she passed a music store and saw an accordion in the window, shiny and red and silver. Of all things in the world Jay wanted an accordion most. Garnet stood a long time looking at it. She felt pleased and proud, as though she had really given it to him.

"Jay and his old strawstack!" she jeered to herself, and bent her head downward because she couldn't help laughing. "My was he cross! Was he ever cross!"

She had a sudden picture of the strawstack capsizing and burying herself; and for some reason it seemed funnier than anything in the world. She walked along with her chin tucked into her collar, trying not to laugh. But she couldn't help it. The laughter swelled and grew stronger, till she shook with it and her breath came in gasps. People looked at her and smiled; and a policeman said: "Sure wish I knew the joke, girly." But after a while the laughing was all used up, and she was able to look about her again and take a deep breath.

Now that she had selected all the things her family most desired she went into the first dime store she saw to buy the presents she could afford.

Garnet loved dime stores and this seemed to be an especially gay and lively one. It was full of people shuffling and pausing and eating candy out of paper sacks. The air was very hot and thick and smelled of perfume and fried onions and chocolate and fly spray. Balloons on stalks blossomed above the toy counter, and there were red and pink crêpe paper decorations wound around the pillars and pinned from wall to wall. Babies cried, mothers called, cash registers jingled briskly, and above the racket, live canaries in cages poured out their song as if this were a gaudy but familiar forest of their own.

At counter twenty-seven a lady was putting cold cream on her face, and talking loud in a voice like an old gramophone record. There was a little crowd of people in front of her, women mostly, holding their bundles loosely and staring.

"This cream," quacked the lady, "is made from the oil of young turtles. Apply it at night just before retiring, and pat in vigorously." Here the lady slapped her face heartily in demonstration. "If used constantly it is guaranteed to remove lines, wrinkles, double chins and freckles, and is beneficial to the tenderest skin."

Her eye fell on Garnet. "Why even a little girl like the one standing there could benefit by the use of this cream. She won't enjoy those freckles when she grows up!" All the women turned their heads together and looked at Garnet, smiling grown-up smiles.

Garnet felt embarrassed. She moved slowly away from the cold cream people, whistling softly between her teeth. Freckles, for goodness' sake! Who cared about freckles?

It took a long time to get presents for her family because she had to look and select and compare. But finally she had most of them. First there was a Wild West book for Jay; and then a little aeroplane for Donald. There was a bandanna handkerchief for her father; and for her mother she found a ring with a red glass jewel in it, bigger and more beautiful than any ruby you ever saw. Only Eric was left. What in the world could she give him?

As she wandered down the aisle with her lumpy looking package of presents, she noticed a sad feeling in her stomach.

"Empty, that's what I am," thought Garnet in surprise. "Empty as a ragpicker's pocket." She remembered Mr. Zangl.

After all it was the middle of the afternoon and she had had no lunch. She paused before a sort of glass cage in which a dozen fat sausages lay toasting on a rack. They smelled good. Better than good.

"One of those please," said Garnet giving a nickel to the sausage lady, who had golden hair and strawberry-colored fingernails.

It came tucked into a roll, with mustard on it. And it was better than good. Nothing is so good as a hot dog at the dime store, thought Garnet. As soon as I finish this I'll have another. And then I'll have some kind of ice cream. And then I'll see.

But just as she had opened her mouth to ask for a second hot dog, a new and dreadful thought occurred to her.

She shook her purse. It sounded quiet; there was no jingle in it. She swallowed and unsnapped the clasp. There was the perfume, yes; and there was the new handkerchief, and the precious thimble. She took them all out and stared into the dark little cave of the pocketbook. Then she held it upside down, but nothing happened. It was empty.

"As a ragpicker's pocket," said Garnet for the second time in ten minutes.

"What's the matter, honey?" asked the sausage lady kindly. "Cleaned out?"

"Cleaned out," echoed Garnet, "and I'm eighteen miles away from home."

The sausage lady had funny thin eyebrows that looked even funnier when she was surprised. She leaned forward to speak; but just then a big woman surrounded by children swept up the counter, puffing.

"Seven," she demanded, "seven hot dogs, please. Two with mustard and five with kraut, and we're in a hurry."

Garnet saw the sausage lady forget all about her, and she went on out of the store.

Well, my goodness, people don't just get lost and starve to death in cities like this, Garnet said to herself. I can hitchhike anyway. It's kind of exciting. I wish Jay was here.

It was queer though. She went on up the street. Her shoes hurt her; and with her aching feet, and her bundle and empty pocketbook she felt like an old, old woman coming home from seeing her grandchildren who didn't love her.

The gates of the little park were open, and Garnet went in. It was nice there, the trees cast a dusty shadow, and the fountain sounded like lemonade. Dozens of people were sitting on the benches and the only space she could find was a very small one between a big man with a newspaper, and a little man with a dog. The newspaper was written in a foreign language, and the dog lifted his lip and sneered when Garnet tried to pat him: so as soon as her feet stopped hurting she went away.

"My, it's noisy," said Garnet to herself. "I'm tired of it. Those trolley cars! They aren't so much."

All the same she would have ridden on one if she had had a nickel. A wave of longing swept over her for her home. No noises there but natural ones, like crickets and cows and roosters in the morning.

Down and down the sloping street she walked; passing again all the windows full of treasure. And over and over she said to herself like a poem:

"A dime for the book and a nickel for the plane;
A dime for father's handkerchief,
A dime for mother's ruby ring."

But then of course she had to add: "And a nickel for a hot dog for me!"

And there was nothing for Eric. Oh she felt ashamed of herself. She should have known better at her age, but that half dollar had looked so big. She had never had all that money to spend before. How disgusted Jay would be! Now there was nothing to do but try to get a free ride home.

Somehow it seemed easier to ask somebody on a country road than right in the middle of a town like this. She walked and walked. The afternoon burned with a deeper light; soon it would be time for supper. Home seemed as far away as Egypt.

The houses grew smaller and shabbier and fewer as she walked, and now she could smell the sweet soft smell of fields. Think of it! In a few hours she had forgotten how they smelled, and how still they were except for the crickets.

Every time a car went by she turned and raised her hand, but always the car whizzed past her scornfully.

The strapped shoes hurt worse and worse, and she was just going to take them off and go barefoot, when she heard another car coming. She straightened up, raising her hand. She saw that it was a truck, with a big load of something.

The truck slowed down and stopped, and the driver looked at Garnet.

"Want a lift, kid?" he asked.

He had a nice kind of face Garnet thought, so she said, "Yes I do!" and climbed in beside him. The air around them was full of cluckings and hen sounds, and when she looked out of the little window behind her head she saw that the truck was loaded with crates of chickens.

"Where are you taking them?" she asked.

"Wholesale market over to Hanson," said the driver. "Each one of them chickens was born and raised to be somebody's Sunday dinner."

"Oh," said Garnet. She didn't look at the chickens again, but she couldn't help hearing them.

"Where are you going, kid?" asked the driver.

90

"I live in a little place called Esau's Valley," she said anxiously. "It's three miles this side of Blaiseville, do you go anywhere near it?"

"Sure do," said the driver reassuringly. "Drive right through it on my way to Hanson."

Oh the good smells of fields in the country! They could have their trolley cars, those city people. Yes, and they could have their green stoves and fur coats, and hot dogs and everything else.

"Been shopping?" asked the driver looking at her bundle.

"I certainly have," said Garnet laughing. "That's why I'm hitchhiking home; I spent every penny I had!"

Then she told him all the things she'd bought, and all about her family.

When they drove down the main street of Hodgeville Garnet heard a sort of crash, and she saw a boy yelling and pointing. She stuck her head out of the window. Behind them there were chickens running all over the street.

"Stop!" shouted Garnet to the driver. "One of the crates fell off and it's broken."

"Them doggone chickens," sighed the driver as he stopped the truck. He sounded as if this had happened to him before. "I tell you I'd rather be hauling a load of wild bull elephants!"

Garnet hopped out too, and began chasing hens. Cars honked and could not pass; heads poked out of upstairs windows, and people stopped on the sidewalk. Hodgeville's one policeman, Gus Winch, appeared from nowhere and gave advice. People laughed and laughed.

Garnet grabbed at and caught a rust-colored hen by its feet. She reached for another on the radiator cap of

a car. The truck driver already had three wildly clucking scrambling bundles of feathers in his arms.

"How many more are out?" panted Garnet, holding
onto the hens.

"Let's see. We've got five; must be one more someplace." The truck driver was very red in the face. He
picked up the broken crate, set it right side up and
dropped the protesting chickens into it. Then he put
another crate on top and ran into a hardware store to
borrow a hammer.

Garnet saw some bushy black tail feathers disappear-
ing into the open door of a furniture store. She ran after
them. What a chase she had! The chicken scrambled
under rocking chairs and flapped noisily over tables
and upholstered sofas. Half a dozen times her fingers
touched its feathers, but each time it got away. Finally
she crawled under a wicker settee in a corner and
caught it. The furniture store man was upset.

"We ain't used to having poultry loose in here," he
complained, and glared at Garnet as though she had
done it on purpose.

Garnet tucked the chicken under her arm, begged
the store man's pardon, and went outside again.

But no sooner was she outdoors than the hen gave
a lurch and a wriggle, and half flying, half running,
went skittering down the street. Hands reached for
it, feet pursued it, but the bad black chicken was a
match for them all. It sped and dodged along the
pavement, clucking furiously, spread its wings and
with a last despairing leap landed heavily on top of
the swinging sign above a restaurant door.

People laughed and laughed. The street echoed with
laughter. The black hen did look funny on its precarious
perch, grumbling and muttering and arranging its

feathers; and printed in red letters on the sign below it were the words: "Chicken Dinners Our Specialty."

"*Now* what in time am I going to do!" said Garnet.

The truck driver ran out of the hardware store with a ladder; and no sooner had he set it against the wall than Garnet was halfway up it with her pigtails flying. She was bound that she would get that chicken. And before the chicken could do more than stand up and cluck and prepare to depart, she had it by the leg.

She looked down triumphantly at the truck driver's face. She felt proud.

"Well here it is," she said. "My goodness, I never saw such a chicken!"

She held it close to her and climbed carefully down the ladder. Now that she had it she felt half sorry that she'd caught it. You couldn't blame a chicken for not wanting to be a dinner.

"Well, by gosh," said the truck driver admiringly, "you sure did a good piece of work that time, kid." And bystanders laughed and congratulated her. She heard an old man saying, "That little girl skinned up that ladder like the devil was after her. Quickest thing I ever seen."

The driver put the chicken in the crate with the others. Then he nailed down the top. Garnet noticed that he left the ends of two laths unnailed.

They got back into the truck again and started off. People waved and called good-bye, still smiling. You could see that they were grateful for having something unexpected to laugh at like that.

It was funny, thought Garnet. This morning Jay had scolded her for doing work badly; and now the truck driver had praised her for doing work well. It sort of made things even.

The driver mopped his hot face with a blue hand-kerchief, and Garnet brushed off her dress. It was dirty from scrambling around after chickens, and there were pecked places on her arms, but she felt wonderful.

"Does this happen often?" she asked politely.

The driver laughed. "Well, not so often," he said. "But once two dozen of my hens got loose in Chicago in the Loop District. Boy, we had city traffic tied up for half an hour. Didn't lose a hen though. Found 'em in buses and barber shops and I don't know what all."

He smiled at Garnet. "They're good hens though. I've won plenty of prizes on 'em up and down the state, and next month I'm going to exhibit them at the New Conniston fair and see what I get."

He reached into his pocket and tossed a little book into Garnet's lap. On the cover was printed:

PREMIUM LIST

Rules and regulations
of the

SOUTHWESTERN
WISCONSIN FAIR

New Conniston, Wisconsin
September 9-10-11-12.

The back cover was more interesting. It said:

SPECIAL ATTRACTIONS

THE GREAT ZORANDER
3   ACTS   3

The most daring and miracu-
lous feats of balance 75 feet
in mid-air. No safety devices!

THE JEWEL GIRLS AND BRUNO
2   acts   2
Two ladies and a man who are
sure to please with acrobatics
and clean comedy

HANK HAZZARD and his HAYSEEDS
Musicians and dancers who
have staggered Broadway with
their versatility.

ALSO many other acts of
distinction and merit too
numerous to name!

Garnet decided not to miss the fair this year if she
could help it; she opened the book and looked at the
list of entries. It seemed as if you could exhibit anything in the world, from cows to cross-stitch, from
swine to sweet pickles!

As she glanced at the livestock lists something caught
her eye: some words in a column under "Class D —

Swine Department." She read: "For best boar under six months, first prize — $3.50, second prize — $1.50."

After all Timmy would be four months old by the ninth of September, and he was certainly the handsomest little pig Garnet had ever seen (thanks to her care). Imagine if he won a prize!

"May I keep this?" she asked.

"Sure thing," said the driver cheerfully. "Are you planning on exhibiting something?"

"A young hog," explained Garnet, and told him about Timmy.

"Well, I hope they pin a ribbon on him for you," said the truck driver. "Sounds like they might, too."

They came into Esau's Valley, now. Garnet's valley too. As long as she lived and wherever she lived this valley would belong to her in a special way because she knew it all by heart.

"Where to, kid?" asked the driver.

"I'll get off at that side road by the mailboxes," said Garnet.

But when she had thanked him and jumped down, she was surprised to see that he too had gotten out and was walking around to the back of the truck.

"Wait a minute, kid," he commanded; he was pulling out the broken crate. Then he swung the two loose-ended laths apart and put his hand in. There was a scuffling and clucking in the crate; and when he brought his hand out again it was holding the bad black chicken by the legs.

"Here's a present for you," said the driver coughing. "I'd never of been able to round up all them hens if it hadn't been for you."

'Oh I *couldn't!*" cried Garnet. But she knew very

well that she could, and that she probably would, because she wanted that chicken terribly.

"Now listen to me," said the truck driver. "You'll be doing me a favor by taking this hen off my hands. She's a born troublemaker and she don't like me. Why I wouldn't be surprised if she pushed that blame crate off the truck all by herself! And I have a feeling she's tough besides and nobody will buy her for Sunday dinner. So how about it?"

"We—ll," said Garnet, and she put her hand out to take the chicken. "Oh you don't know how glad I am to have her! I hated to think of her on a platter with mashed potatoes and gravy."

"Okay, kid. So long," said the driver, jumping into his truck. And before she could thank him properly, or say good-bye, he was half a mile away in a cloud of dust.

Garnet held the chicken under her arm. Now after all she had a present to give to Eric, and one that he would like better than anything else; a live thing that belonged to himself alone, that he could feed and take care of and build a little house for.

"Nobody will eat you, poor chicken," said Garnet to the hen, who looked tired and dejected, with her red comb drooping.

The road was striped with late afternoon tree shadows. She saw someone walking towards her; it was Mr. Freebody.

"Hello, Mr. Freebody," shouted Garnet, but she couldn't wave because of the bundle in one arm and the hen in the other. And she couldn't run to meet him because her shoes hurt her so badly.

"Look at my chicken, Mr. Freebody!" said Garnet, "and look at my bundle. It's all presents!"

Mr. Freebody didn't say anything.

"I hitchhiked too, just like Eric," she continued.

Still Mr. Freebody didn't say anything. It was queer. Garnet looked at him.

"Are you mad, Mr. Freebody?" she asked.

Mr. Freebody was silent for a second or two longer; then he said, "Garnet, it's a funny thing. I ain't related to you in any way. But I've known your mama since she was littler than you. And I've known your dad longer than that; and you folks having a farm right next to mine and all of us being good friends has made me feel like I'm an uncle to you or a granddad or something of the sort. And I've had more worry from you than any young-one I ever knew. Why you wasn't more'n a year old when I took a safety pin out of your mouth. When you was about three I hauled you out of the crick all muddy and half-drowned. When you was a little older than that you climbed up a tree in my orchard and couldn't get down again; I had to fetch you down with a ladder. And then when that mean bull over to Hausers' got after you, who was it pulled you over the pasture fence by the skirt of your dress? I did. And who gave you mustard and water when you et a bite out of that big pink toadstool you found in the woods? I did. And who picked you up and took you to the doctor the time you fell off that heifer you thought you could ride on? I did. Yes, and not so long ago you had us all scared white-haired when you and that little Hauser girl got locked in the liberry. Now. Here you get all upset over a squabble with Jay and off you go hitchhiking to the Lord knows where."

"To New Conniston," said Garnet in a small voice. This was terrible.

98

"All right, New Conniston," said Mr. Freebody. "Eighteen miles away all by yourself, without a word to no one. I knew you was up to mischief when I saw you had shoes on. And that dress."

"Is mother worried about me?" asked Garnet.

"No she ain't," said Mr. Freebody unexpectedly. "Matter of fact nobody's worried about you but me. They've been too busy. Your dad thought you was home and your mama thought you was out to the threshing or with the Hauser girl. You said you didn't want dinner so nobody bothered about that. Nope, ain't nobody worried about you but me. And if I was you I wouldn't say nothing about your little jaunt for the time being; no sense in getting your mama upset now that you've been and done it."

"But my presents!" wailed Garnet.

"Presents can wait," said Mr. Freebody sternly. "In a couple of days when things are quieter, you can bring 'em out and tell your mama how you got 'em."

"Oh Mr. Freebody," said Garnet. "I'm sorry I'm such a nuisance to you. I wish I didn't do things the way I do."

Suddenly she held the chicken out to him.

"Please would you hold her for a minute?" She sat down at the roadside. "I just *have* to take these shoes off."

Mr. Freebody held the hen and laughed.

"I guess it ain't no use," he said. "I never saw a young-one with spirit that didn't get into mischief from time to time. You're pretty well-behaved on the whole; I wouldn't have you different. Just *think* a little oftener, that's all I mean. We don't want anything to happen to you."

Garnet felt better. The dust was soft as velvet under her feet, and she could feel each one of her toes rejoicing. Mr. Freebody promised to keep the hen for her till she could give it to Eric.

"What shall I name her?" asked Garnet.

"I ain't much hand at naming things," said Mr. Freebody. "I've always had a horse named Beauty, and I've always had a dog named Major, but I ain't never had a hen named anything. Let's see now. How about Blackie?"

Garnet shook her head slowly.

"I don't think that's quite the right name for her," she replied. "This hen is different from other hens; she has a lot of fighting spirit. There was a goddess once who was a sort of warrior; mother told me about her. But what was her name? I can't remember."

"And I can't help you," said Mr. Freebody.

They went through the gate and Mr. Freebody went out to the chicken coops to hide the chicken, and Garnet went down to the cold room to hide her bundle. All the time she kept trying to remember the name of the goddess.

At supper everyone was very tired and had oats in their hair and talked about threshing, and how many sacks they'd got, and what a good quality the oats were.

Afterwards Garnet dried dishes. While she was putting plates in the china cupboard Jay came up to her and said: "As soon as you're finished let's go into town. Mr. Freebody'll take us in and we can catch a ride back with someone. There's a band concert tonight, and we can get some pop or something."

"Okay, let's! Tell Eric too," said Garnet. She smiled at Jay. She knew that he felt a little sorry for the way he'd spoken to her in the field. But he would never tell her so in words; and it didn't matter.

"Brünnhilde!" she shouted suddenly.

Jay just looked at her. "What in time are you talking about now?"

"There was a goddess who was sort of a warrior," explained Garnet. "She had a helmet and spear and everything, and I just remembered what she was called. I wanted to name something after her."

"Are you ever goofy!" sighed Jay. "Well, come on, hurry up. I'll help you finish these."

And afterwards Garnet and Jay and Eric went in to town. It was wonderful.

Lots of people were there because it was Wednesday, the day that farmers bring their cattle in to sell and ship away.

The band played in a sort of screened cage set up on stilts over a street corner. They played loud, cheerful music, and they all had their coats off because they got so hot playing it.

Garnet and Eric and Jay walked up and down the street and talked to their friends. They stopped and watched a bingo game for a while, and then they went up in the band-concert thing, and the drummer let Jay beat his drum during one entire waltz. All Jay had to do was to go: *Boom* thump-thump, *Boom* thump-thump, over and over again, with a big thundery crash on the *Boom* and two gentle bounces on the thump-thump. Jay would have liked to go on playing waltzes all night, but Garnet and Eric wanted him to come down with them, and anyway the drummer said the next number was to be a march, and much too difficult for Jay. After that they bought some ice-cream cones, and after that they drank pop out of bottles. And then they got some peanuts in a bag, and walked up the street eating them, and scattering shells and laughing; and everything was all right again.

VIII. Fair Day

O N THE ninth of September the sun came up with
a special glory. The air was deep and clear and
full of blue light the way it often is in September, and
now and then the wind moved a little. There was a huge
feeling about this wind though it moved so slightly;
it was as if it came from far away, through a door that
was open into another space.

Garnet woke up early. Before she was quite wide
awake she lay with her eyes closed, half afraid to look
for fear it might be raining. But even with them closed
she knew it was going to be all right because the color
behind her lids was clear and rosy and she knew the
sunlight lay upon them. And she heard crickets in the
meadow, and a fly buzzing against the screen, and
somebody whistling outside. So it *was* all right and
she opened her eyes. Oh what a day! She held up her
arm in the sunlight; all the little hairs on it glittered

like fine gold, and her closed fingers were ember-colored as if there were a light inside them.

She kicked off the blankets and pointed her foot into the sunlight, and her toes were ember-colored too, though not so much as her fingers.

She yawned and stretched and gave a sudden leap that brought her out of bed. Without waiting to put on a bathrobe she ran out of the room and down the stairs which were uncarpeted and hollow sounding, like drums.

Bang! went the screen door at the bottom, and Garnet was halfway across the lawn; racing towards a small pen that stood by itself. Eric had built it especially for Timmy.

"Timmy!" called Garnet, "Lazy Timmy, it's time to get up!" But Timmy had been awake for ages and came lolloping over to the fence rail looking interested and hungry. He was quite big now, and his coat was very stiff and fine; he stood well and looked as if he could take care of himself no matter what happened. Every day for several weeks Garnet had been training him to walk and stand like a prize hog. Mr. Freebody had showed her how to steer him along with two little boards, and how to make him stand neatly with his two front hoofs together.

Garnet scratched Timmy's back with a twig, and he leaned against the fence with his little eyes half closed, grunting softly with pleasure.

"Today you must remember everything I've taught you," Garnet told him. "You are going for a long ride in a little crate that you won't like much. And then you'll be taken into a big sort of shed and put into a pen by yourself; but there'll be lots of other pens there with pigs in them too. So you can make friends and not be lonesome. Then by-and-by some men will come and look at you and you must walk right and stand right just the way I showed you, and maybe you'll win a lovely blue ribbon."

Timmy twitched his little tail that was all curled up like a pretzel; then he rolled over on his back so that she could scratch his stomach.

"Garnet!" called Mrs. Linden from the house. "You come in and get dressed this minute!"

It *was* rather chilly with nothing on but a nightgown. Garnet wrapped her arms around her cold self and hurried to the house.

"Will he win a prize, mother, do you think?" she asked.

"I shouldn't wonder, darling," said her mother, "he's a changed pig since you took him in hand."

Garnet went up to her room and dressed with care. She put on the blue dress and shoes. (But not the strapped ones; those she would never wear again!) She braided her pigtails so tight they hurt her, and scrubbed her face till it had a shine like shellac. Then she went down to the kitchen where she could hear bacon hissing and sputtering in the frying pan.

The whole family was going to the fair, and they were all dressed up for the occasion. Jay and Eric both had straight hair for once; they had used so much water on it that there were little trickles at the back of their necks; and Donald had to eat his breakfast in one of Mrs. Linden's aprons so that he would be sure to leave the table without oatmeal decorations. Garnet thought her mother looked wonderful; she had on a flowered dress, and her hair was different.

Mr. Linden looked fine, too, in a dark suit and a collar that hurt him.

Garnet's stomach felt as if there were a pinwheel inside of it turning and spinning a shower of sparks. She said so to her mother.

"It's excitement," said Mrs. Linden calmly, "excitement and emptiness. Eat your cereal." "Oh *mother!*" groaned Garnet, "I *can't.*" "Yes you can, darling," insisted her mother heartlessly. "You can't leave the house till you've finished every spoonful." Garnet ploughed through the cereal grimly.

"It's like eating Boulder Dam," she grumbled, but she finished it. Then she leapt from her chair and started for the door; and then came slowly, sadly back.

"The dishes," she said. "Oh, let them stand for once!" cried Mrs. Linden grandly, "we can do them when we come home. This is an important day."

"You're nice," said Garnet, and gave her mother a hug.

Eric called through the window, "Come on Garnet, Mr. Freebody's here with his truck, let's get Timmy in his box."

"Poor pig!" said Garnet to Timmy, who struggled and rolled his eyes and squealed when they put him in the crate. "But just think if you win a prize!"

"That little hog don't care nothing about blue ribbons, I bet," said Mr. Freebody, "a couple of square feet of mud and a full trough and he'd be a durn sight more contented." Mr. Freebody laughed. "He sure looks pretty as a peach though, don't he? Smells good, too. How did that happen?"

"Oh, I washed him," said Garnet. "The soap smelled like that."

"My, my what a fancy little hog!" chuckled Mr. Freebody. "With all them clean bristles and that fine smell of perfumery I'm going to be mighty disappointed in the Fair Authorities if he don't get a prize!"

Mr. Freebody had offered to drive his truck to New Conniston solely for Timmy's convenience. The Linden's didn't have a truck and there wasn't enough room in the Ford for both the family and Timmy's crate.

"But I'm going to ride in the truck with you, Mr. Freebody," Garnet told him.

"Just so's you can keep on eye on that pig, I bet," said Mr. Freebody, "well get in then. It's time we started."

Garnet watched the precious crate safely installed on the back of the truck; then she got in herself. She called good-bye to her family who were busily getting themselves sorted out and into the Ford. This was particularly difficult as Mrs. Hauser, her daughter Citronella and her son Hugo had just arrived and wanted to go with them.

"It's a good thing you decided to come with me," remarked Mr. Freebody, "otherwise I don't know how you *would* have got to the fair, or Timmy either. Them Hausers are a mighty fleshy family."

Garnet watched Mrs. Hauser get into the car. Did she imagine it, or did she really see the Ford sink down a little on its springs, as if it sighed under a great weight. My goodness, thought Garnet, Mother, Father, Jay, Donald, Eric, *and* Mrs. Hauser, *and* Hugo, *and* —

"Citronella!" shouted Garnet, "you come ride with us. There's lots of room, isn't there Mr. Freebody?"

"*Always* room for one more," said Mr. Freebody

gallantly, leaning across Garnet to open the door for Citronella.

Garnet squirmed around to peer through the window at Timmy in his box.

"He looks as if he had hurt feelings," she said. "He'll probably never forgive me for this."

"Just try giving him something to eat and see how he'll come around," said Mr. Freebody, "Hogs are only sensitive between meals."

By this time the truck was halfway down the side road.

"My, I was awful scared I wasn't going to get to go to the fair at all," said Citronella. "Merle took the car to Hanson to get the springs fixed, and Cicero and Dad and Uncle Ed took our Holstein bull to the fair in the stake truck. Wasn't anything left for us but the team till Mama thought of asking you folks."

"It's a good day for a fair," remarked Mr. Freebody, " 't ain't cold, 't ain't hot, and not a cloud in sight."

"Do you think he's warm enough?" asked Garnet.

"Who?" said Mr. Freebody, "Timmy? He's warm, don't you worry."

When they came to Hodgeville, Mr. Freebody stopped the truck.

"How about some ice-cream cones?" he asked.

"It's a fine idea," said Garnet.

"It's a marvelous idea," said Citronella.

So Mr. Freebody went into a drugstore and got a maple-nut ice-cream cone for Citronella, and a chocolate ice-cream cone for Garnet, and a plain vanilla one for himself. But for Timmy he bought a strawberry one and let Garnet poke it between the laths of the crate. Timmy's snout trembled all around the edges with joy, and in a second he had gobbled every crumb. He looked less miserable.

"He knows you ain't betrayed him anyhow," Mr. Freebody told Garnet.

Citronella just stood looking at them.

"Giving ice cream to a pig," she said, and gave her cone a long, thoughtful lick. "To a *pig!*" she repeated and gave it another lick. "My land, what a waste!" she said.

"I'm doing lots of awful things today," said Garnet complacently. "Leaving the dishes, feeding ice-cream cones to pigs, and eating one myself at nine o'clock in the morning!"

"Won't hurt you once in a while," said Mr. Freebody and they all got back in the truck and slammed the doors.

On they drove through the burning blue day. There was no haze on the hills, no mist on the river. Everything was clear as crystal. They passed Melody, and Garnet remembered the people on the bus, and the wonderful ride after the people got off, and how she'd bounced around on the seat and tried not to scream.

She looked back at Timmy. He was lying down.

"Do you think he's all right?" she asked.

"Who?" said Mr. Freebody, "Timmy? He's fine, never felt better."

Garnet looked at Mr. Freebody out of the corners of her eyes and laughed.

"You understand pigs pretty well, don't you Mr. Freebody" she remarked.

"Sure do," said he. "Ought to. Raised enough of 'em!"

Now they could see New Conniston on its hill. Garnet felt the pinwheel in her stomach again.

They drove past the little shabby homes, and on through the main street with its big important stores and the dime store where Garnet had bought her presents; past the park with the fountain and on to the outskirts of the city where the fairgrounds were.

Then they drove through the wide gates into the new, gay world of the fair, which, like a magic city in a story, had sprung up over night.

It was a whirling, jingling, bewildering collection of noise and color and smell. Everything seemed to be spinning and turning; merry-go-rounds, the Ferris wheel, the whip cars. There were dozens of tents with peaked tops and scalloped edges, and little colored flags flying from them. Citronella grabbed Garnet and Garnet grabbed Citronella, and they bounced up and down shrieking with excitement. Mr. Freebody was calmer. "I always like a fair," he said.

They drove directly to the stock pavilions and stopped in front of the one that was labeled SWINE in big black letters.

The man in charge of it was fat and kind looking. His name was Fred Lembke. He and Mr. Freebody carried the crate in, opened it, and put Timmy in a nice clean pen with hay on the floor. "He doesn't feel at home yet," said Garnet apologetically to Mr. Lembke, because Timmy just stood where he had been set down, looking insulted and loathing everything.

"He's a mighty fine little boar, just the same," said Mr. Lembke with real admiration in his voice (not just the nice-to-children sort). "Who's showing him?"

"I am," replied Garnet, feeling very motherly towards Timmy.

Mr. Lembke took a notebook from his pocket and a

pencil from behind his ear and asked Garnet her name, and all about Timmy. Then he put a sign above Timmy's pen that said:

Class 36: Boar under 6 months.

Breed: Hampshire.

Owner: Garnet Linden.

Garnet read the sign over three or four times to herself. Then she turned to Mr. Freebody. "Am I supposed to stay and watch him?" she asked.

"No, no," replied Mr. Freebody. "You two little girls go on out and enjoy yourselves. You've got hours before the judges come. Three o'clock they'll be here, and see that you get back in time!"

"I don't know how I'll ever wait till three o'clock," sighed Garnet, but in the next minute she had forgotten all about time and waiting. There were dozens, hundreds of things to see and do.

First they looked at all the other pigs in the shed. There were several others in Timmy's class, some bigger than he, and some more important looking. Garnet and Citronella examined each one with anxiety.

"Well anyway," said Garnet, "I bet Timmy's got the nicest nature." "He's the handsomest, too," said Citronella stoutly.

The place was full of pigs. There were many different breeds with high sounding names like Poland-China, Chester White, and Duroc-Jersey. There were grumpy looking hogs, and sows with litters of pigs all different sizes. In one pen there was a whole group of baby ones fast asleep; white as thistledown, they were, with pale pink ears and little turned-up snouts. It didn't seem possible that they would someday grow up to be boisterous, bellowing, bad mannered pigs. In another pen,

111

near the front of the shed, there was a prize hog, black and thundery, and big as a grand piano. On the sign above him were pinned the ribbons from past fairs, all blue!

The whole shed resounded with the snorts, grunts, squeals and grumblings of pigs conversing.

"How rude they sound," said Garnet, "as if they never said nice things to each other, but just scolded, and snatched, and told each other to get out of the way."

The cattle pavilion seemed very quiet and respectable after that. There was almost no noise. Cows stood in stalls on either side of the shed, with soft, dull eyes, and jaws moving patiently. There were little calves with pink noses, and magnificent, dangerous-looking bulls.

Garnet and Citronella stopped in front of the Hausers' Holstein, staring admiringly. He was massive and beautiful, with his shining black-and-white coat.

Mr. Hauser came and stood beside them with his hands in his pockets.

"Looks pretty good, don't he?" he remarked.

"He chased me once," said Garnet rather proudly. "I was pretty scared."

"Yes, and who saved you *that* time?" asked someone, giving one of her pigtails a jerk. Garnet turned around. Of course it was Mr. Freebody.

"You won't ever have to do it again," she promised.

"Looks like you couldn't lose, Herman," said Mr. Freebody to Mr. Hauser, and the two girls went on to look at the horses.

There were stallions in big stalls there, roan, and dapple-grey and black. They had huge arched necks and dark fiery eyes. Their hoofs made a heavy, restless noise upon the floorboards. And there was a little colt that was hard to leave. He had a satiny coat, and long unreliable legs that he could fold up like jack-knives. He looked delicate and mischievous standing by the strong, protecting shape of his mother.

"If he was mine I'd name him Ariel," said Garnet stroking his nose. Oh, how soft his nose was! Like moss, like velvet, like the palm of a baby's hand.

"Of course it might not suit him when he grew up," she added thoughtfully. "Ariel's a funny name anyway. Like on a radio. I don't see what it's got to do with a horse," said Citronella. "If he was mine I'd name him Black Beauty like the book."

"But he's not black," objected Garnet. "Well, it's a good name for a horse," said Citronella.

Finally they tore themselves away, and left the dim sheds where the air had a heavy smell of hay and animals, and went out into the blaze and flourish of the fair.

IX. Ice-Cream Cones and Blue Ribbons

THEY crossed a smooth dirt track that lay in a large oval enclosing the central section of the fair. Later in the day there would be trotting races on this track, and there would be crowds of excited people at either side, but now it was just a kind of road to be crossed.

They simply wandered for a while, pausing to look at the shies, and the shooting gallery, and the screaming people in the whip cars. They bought two ice-cream cones and poked along, stopping to read the signs outside of the tents that you had to pay to go into. There were a lot of them, all interesting. Aurora the Mystic Mind Reader. Professor Hedwitz, World Famous Phrenologist. Hercules Junior, the Samson of the Century. Dagmar, the Female Sword Swallower. Zara, the Jungle Dancer. Below the last name, Zara, there was a little notice saying: persons under 16 not admitted. Both Garnet and Citronella were dying to know why not. There were many other tents and sideshows but it was still too early in the day for them to be open, and those loud-voiced men who usually shout outside and take the money, had not yet appeared.

The flaps of the tent announcing Dagmar, the Female Sword Swallower, were open, and inside Garnet and Citronella saw a woman in a kimona sitting on a chair and darning a sock. She was chewing gum.

"Do you think it's her?" whispered Citronella as they went on.

"It *can't* be!" said Garnet. "I'm sure a sword swallower would look, you know, *different*. Not so much like other people. Wilder."

"I bet it is though!" persisted Citronella. "Maybe she *has* to chew gum," she added, "to keep her jaws limber or something. In order to swallow swords."

They went back to take another peek but this time the woman noticed them, and though she smiled, she closed the tent flaps.

"I bet it's her all right." said Citronella excitedly. This was something to have seen, a real lady sword swallower darning socks just like anyone!

The merry-go-round looked wonderful. It was the kind that has only horses, not wild animals; but they were strange beautiful horses with flaring scarlet nostrils and broad grins. Garnet and Citronella each paid a nickel and got on. After a while the music commenced and the merry-go-round began turning. Up went the horses, high, swooping in the air as they glided, and then down like winged horses following the wind.

"I'm kind of old for this," remarked Citronella, who was eleven. "But I still like it."

"I'm never going to be too old for it," said Garnet. "All my life whenever I see a merry-go-round I'm going to ride on it, and when I have children I'm going to ride with them."

They had two more rides and then they got off, and continued their exploring. They got some popcorn, too, and then they had a ride on the whip-cars. It was perfect. Their necks were nearly snapped in half, and all the little bones in their spinal columns kept feeling as if they were flying apart and then settling back in place again like something in a movie of Mickey Mouse.

"Oh, gee!" squealed Citronella as they rounded a curve with a particularly terrifying wallop. "Isn't this awful?"

"But fun!" squealed Garnet in reply, and clutched Citronella as they rounded another curve.

They got off feeling very light and peculiar in their feet and rather whirly in their heads, and they went straight to a hot dog stand where they each bought and ate two hot dogs and a bottle of root beer.

"How about the Ferris wheel, now?" enquired Garnet, ready for anything.

"Let's wait a little bit," urged Citronella in a careful voice. She looked rather green around the mouth. "I don't feel so good," she said.

"Just don't think about it and you'll be all right," advised Garnet airily, not having a stomach ache herself.

They decided to go and see the cooking and needle-work exhibits in the big barnlike building at the far end of the fair. Hundreds of people had arrived by this time and Garnet caught a glimpse of her mother and Mrs. Hauser with Donald and Hugo.

"Don't say anything about feeling sick," Garnet cautioned Citronella. "They might think you should go home!"

"I feel better now, anyway," said Citronella, breathing a great sigh of relief. It was wonderful to know that she wasn't going to be sick after all; the fair took on a new color and beauty because of it.

"Oh I feel swell!" she cried joyously and gave a sudden skip.

They went into the barnlike building and looked at everything. There were hundreds of jars of jelly and pickles on the shelves, there were cut flowers in vases and growing plants in pots. In one of the glass cases there were dozens of different kinds of cake; golden cake, and marble, and fruit cake and orange; angel food and devil food and sponge! Each had a little card beside it with the name of the lady who'd made it.

"Oh, how delicious they look," moaned Garnet. "Oh how my mouth is watering!"

"Mine isn't," said Citronella. "I still don't feel so good when I look at those cakes."

So they went on to the needlework section. Here they saw rag rugs and braid, and hook rugs, and baby clothes, and children's clothes, and crocheted afghans, and quilts, and sofa cushions embroidered with flowers and big dog's heads and other beautiful things.

Garnet heard someone say, "Why there's that little hitchhiker we picked up over to Esau's Valley!"

118

She turned around, and sure enough, there was Mrs. Zangl in a big lavender dress and a hat with a rose on it; and behind her with his hand on her shoulder stood Mr. Zangl, that nice, nice man. Garnet was glad to see them. They shook hands all around and said what a fine fair it was, and Citronella was introduced.

"Are you exhibiting a quilt today?" Garnet asked Mrs. Zangl.

"Look at that," said Mr. Zangl, waving his outstretched hand towards a quilt hanging on the wall. "Just take a good look at that. See what the judges thought of it."

Garnet looked at Mrs. Zangl's quilt; so did Citronella. It was every color in the world almost; all made of patches put together like flowers in a garden. It was the gayest, most brilliant coverlet you could ever hope to sleep under. There was a big blue ribbon pinned to the card with Mrs. Zangl's name on it.

"Beautiful!" said Garnet.

"Just beautiful!" said Citronella.

"Just the colors alone would keep you warm," said Garnet.

Mrs. Zangl's gold tooth glittered.

"It's real nice of you to say so," she smiled. "I always did like plenty of color. My, I felt bad when I got too fleshy to wear red dresses! I guess I take it out of my system by making my quilts so bright and all."

"How about ice-cream cones for you three girls?" asked Mr. Zangl heartily.

"Well—" said Garnet looking at Citronella —

"Well—" said Citronella looking at Garnet. "I don't believe just *one* more would hurt me if I ate it real slow. I feel fine now," she added in a whisper.

119

So they all had ice-cream cones. And Citronella ate every crumb of hers; she was entirely cured.

Then they thanked Mr. and Mrs. Zangl and promised to come and call if they ever came over to Deepwater; and Mr. Zangl said that he would come and take a look at Timmy later on.

As the two girls walked back among the tents and sideshows they noticed some people coming out of the one belonging to Zara, the Jungle Dancer (persons under 16 not admitted). Among them was a boy. It was Eric.

"Well!" said Garnet going up to him and hooking onto his arm so he couldn't get away.

"Yes, *well!"* echoed Citronella.

"When did you have your sixteenth birthday, Eric *darling!"* mocked Garnet.

"Maybe he can't read yet," taunted Citronella. "Maybe he's too young!"

Eric was unruffled. He just grinned and licked the long black licorice stick he was carrying.

"Oh I just took a big breath and stretched myself up and out. Then I looked straight ahead and gave my money to the man in that pulpit-thing and in I went. Anyway lots of kids are young looking for their age."

"Yes, but Eric, what was *inside?"* asked Garnet prancing along beside him.

"Something scary, I bet," said Citronella hopefully.

"Aw, it wasn't worth ten cents at all," said Eric disappointingly. "It was just kind of a stout lady in a grass skirt. She had long hair and a lot of bracelets, and she did a sort of dance. You know, like this — " He tried, with much wiggling, to imitate the jungle dancer. Garnet and Citronella were delighted.

120

They walked on looking at things and talking. Suddenly Eric began to laugh at something he was remembering.

"You know what?" said he. "That lady, that Zara, the jungle dancer; she had a pair of glasses on, the kind that pinch to the bridge of your nose; she must have forgotten to take 'em off. Did she ever look funny!"

They found Mrs. Linden and Donald sitting in the shade of one of the tents. They looked exhausted.

"Donald's been on everything he could ride on in this whole fair," said Mrs. Linden. "All except the whip cars and the Ferris wheel, and I won't let him go on those."

"Ponies — " bragged Donald, "I rode on real live ponies around a ring, and I was on the big merry-go-round and the little merry-go-round and that thing like a train." He looked at his mother. "But I *want* to go on the whip cars, and I *want* to go on the Ferris wheel."

"No," said Mrs. Linden automatically. She had been saying it for hours about those two particular things.

"Come with me, Donald," said Eric, "we'll go and see the little pigs, and the fine horses, and maybe we can find a balloon for you, someplace." He took Donald's hand and led him away.

"I don't know how we ever got along without Eric," sighed Mrs. Linden fanning herself with her pocketbook.

"Where are Jay and father?" asked Garnet.

"Your father's still looking at the farm machinery," Mrs. Linden said, "and Jay's been in the shies throwing tennis balls at china teapots for hours."

Mrs. Hauser came towards them puffing like a locomotive. She was very hot; there were dew drops on her upper lip and her big nice face was the color of the rising sun. Under her arm she carried two huge pink Kewpie dolls; one with a red ballet skirt and one with green.

"I won 'em," said Mrs. Hauser, grunting as she let herself carefully and gradually sink to the ground. "One at the coconut shy and one at the weight-lifting thing. You'd think they'd have better prizes than Kewpie dolls! Garnet, you can have the green one, and Citronella can keep the red. My, how my arches pain me."

"It's almost time for the stock judging, Garnet," warned Mrs. Linden, "you have about a half an hour."

"I know what let's do, we just have time," said Garnet. "How do you feel about the Ferris wheel now, Citronella?"

"I feel fine about it now," said Citronella.

So they went to the little booth by the Ferris wheel and paid their money, and when it stopped they got on and sat side by side in a little hanging seat with a bar in front to keep them from falling out.

The operator pulled a big lever and the wheel gave a lurch and a creak, and up they went backwards, with the earth and the fair dropping away from them like a vanishing world. It was rather terrifying but exciting too. When they came to the top they could see the tents and surrounding fields and houses of New Conniston all spread out and flat and strange. And then they went down again like going over Niagara Falls in a barrel, and then up again like being shot out of a gun.

The third time around just as they reached the top

the wheel stopped, and all the little suspended seats rocked to and fro sickeningly.

"They're just letting some more people on probably," said Citronella reassuringly, and they leaned over the bar and looked down, down. But nobody was getting on. They saw the operator's bent-over back below them. He pulled the lever and the wheel gave a quiver but didn't move. They watched him jerk the lever back and forth angrily, push his hat to the back of his head and wipe his forehead. Then he looked up.

"Nothing to worry about, folks," he called, "just a temporary delay."

"He means it's stuck," groaned Citronella. "Oh, gee!"

"And it's almost time for Timmy and the judges, Oh dear!" said Garnet.

Looking down like that gave you an awful feeling. Garnet held onto the side of the seat and raised her eyes. Below and on all sides lay the fair, whirling and jingling and unconcerned. She had never seen a ladder high enough to reach to the top of the Ferris wheel. It made her feel queer to think of that.

"We get stuck in the worst places," grumbled Citronella, "libraries and Ferris wheels!"

"Oh, well they'll get it fixed soon," said Garnet hopefully.

But the Ferris wheel was stuck for more than half an hour.

There they were at the top of the world, or so it felt, and nothing could be done. The sun beat down unmercifully, and now and then the cool, wide September air moved about them like cold currents at the bottom of a stream.

"There's Jay," said Citronella.

And sure enough, looking small and unimportant down there on the ground, stood Jay with his hands cupped to his mouth.

"Hey!" he yelled. "It's three o'clock! Hurry up!" They could barely hear him but guessed at his meaning when he pointed repeatedly at the watch in his hand.

"Maybe he thinks we should just spread our wings and fly," said Citronella acidly. She was thirsty.

Jay stared up at them helplessly, and then went over to talk to the operator of the wheel. After he had spoken with him he looked up at the girls again and hunched his shoulders. "Nothing doing yet awhile," he shouted. "We'll send your dinner up by carrier pigeons." Then he laughed heartily and went away. He walked fast with his legs opening and shutting like a pair of scissors. Lucky Jay, thought Garnet. Lucky Jay, with two legs walking firmly on the firm earth.

"Awful funny, isn't he?" said Citronella sulkily.

"Oh, we'll be down soon, don't you worry," comforted Garnet. She looked about her at the people in the other seats. In back of them was a man all by himself, reading a newspaper which he had thoughtfully provided. And in front a man and a girl were writing notes on bits of paper and tossing them down to friends below, amid screams of laughter. Nobody seemed worried.

Just then the wheel shuddered and moved forward. Everyone had had enough of it by this time, and Garnet and Citronella had to wait while it stopped five times to let the people off who were ahead of them.

"Hurry!" commanded Garnet grabbing Citronella by the hand and running, "we've got to get to Timmy!"

"Oh land!" groaned Citronella, loping along and whacking into people. "I'm just about dying for a drink of water!"

"Afterwards," promised Garnet, "barrels of water afterwards. Come on, *do* hurry!"

But when they got to the track crossing there was a bar in front of the gate and an important looking guard beside it.

"Take it easy, now," he said to the girls as they pushed their way through the crowd to the rail. "There's a race going on. You'll have to wait till it's over."

Dust rose from the track as horses trotted past; sunlight glittered on the spokes of wheels.

"I never knew a race to be so slow!" complained Garnet, hopping up and down and wringing her hands. "Oh *dear*, I can't bear it."

"Never mind," said Citronella. It was her turn to be comforting. "I'm real glad of a rest, we'll get there pretty soon."

Finally it was over. The guard lifted the bar and they went through. They never knew what horse won the race, nor did they care. They were running a kind of race themselves.

They dashed into the pavilion and Garnet pushed her way past people to Mr. Freebody whom she saw standing by Timmy's pen.

"Are we too late?" she gasped almost in tears.

Mr. Freebody motioned with his broad hand towards Timmy's card above the pen.

"The judges have been and went," he said solemnly.

"Oh dear — !" began Garnet, and then she saw what he was pointing at. A blue ribbon it was. A *blue* ribbon! Pinned to Timmy's card.

"Oh," said Garnet, for a moment speechless. Then she began leaping up and down. "Oh wonderful!" she shouted. "Oh, Mr. Freebody, how *wonderful!*" And she climbed right over the railing into Timmy's pen and gave him a good squeeze around the middle.

"Darling Timmy, aren't you proud of yourself?" she said. Timmy let out a stifled grunt.

"He's got his vanity same's the rest of us," commented Mr. Freebody leaning his arms on the railing. "Don't you go spoiling him now, or you'll have one of them temperamental hogs on your hands. He's had plenty of attention for one day, come on out of that pen and let's all go and celebrate."

Garnet climbed reluctantly over the railing. Timmy didn't care; he lay down comfortably on his side with his hoofs crossed, sighed deeply, and fell asleep.

Mr. and Mrs. Linden came towards them through the crowd, they had been searching everywhere for Garnet. Behind them came Mrs. Hauser. She had two balloons, one shaped like Mickey Mouse and one shaped like a Zeppelin. She also carried a cut glass bowl and half a dozen wax fruit to put into it which she had won in a bingo game.

"Did you see what happened to Timmy?" cried Garnet hurling herself upon her parents.

"We were there when the judges came, darling," replied her mother. "We watched him being shown."

"My goodness," said Garnet abruptly. "Who did show him?" She hadn't thought of that before.

"Who do you think?" said someone behind her giving one of her pigtails a jerk. Garnet didn't need to turn around to know who it was. Of course it was Mr. Freebody again. Naturally.

"Oh dear," said Garnet, "Poor Mr. Freebody, always saving my life."

Mr. Freebody laughed.

"Well you couldn't help it this time," he comforted her. "I saw you settin' up there in that little basket with Citronella, and I says to myself, we'll just have to do without her. I said so to the little hog too, and he told me 'Okay.' "

"You've done a fine job with Timmy," said her father putting his arm around her shoulders, "maybe you'll grow up to be the farmer in this family. Jay doesn't seem to have much taste for it, and I think Donald's going to be a G-man."

"How about Eric?" asked Garnet.

"Eric may not want to stay with us always," answered her father. "But I wish he would."

"I do too," agreed Garnet. Eric was part of the family now, a brother. It would be awful if he ever left.

"There he is now," said her father.

Eric had Donald on his shoulders, and Hugo Hauser at his side. Donald had a balloon and a tin horn, and Hugo had a bag of peanuts and a flag. They all looked dirty but pleased.

Garnet told Eric about Timmy and he had to go and see the blue ribbon for himself.

"Do they have prizes for hens?" he enquired. "Next year I think I'll show Brünnhilde!"

"Where's Jay?" asked Garnet. Where was Jay? She did want him to see Timmy in all his glory. She couldn't enjoy her triumph fully without him.

"Well doggone if I didn't almost forget," said Mr. Freebody suddenly. "Here it is Garnet." He fished in his pocket, "your prize money. Three brand new dollar bills *and* a fifty cent piece."

Garnet was dazzled by such wealth. She folded the crisp bills thoughtfully and put them into her pocketbook.

"Whatever will you do with it all?" asked Citronella rather enviously.

"First," said Garnet, "I will have a party. Tonight I'm going to buy everybody's supper. And after that — well, I haven't decided."

But she thought to herself: I will just keep it for a while, sometime I'll want it for something really important. Maybe at Christmas time; or maybe the next time I find bills in the mailbox. Or I wonder how much a second-hand accordion would cost?

"I'm going to look for Jay," Garnet told her family and her friends, and slipped out of the shed into the mellowing sunlight of the late afternoon.

She almost bumped into him a few minutes later; he had a box under his arm and was hurrying.

"Jay!" said Garnet. "Timmy got first prize!"

"I know," said Jay. "I saw him get it. Look, I won something for you. A present, because of Timmy."

Oh Jay was wonderful, Garnet thought, ripping the string and paper from the box with eager fingers. She decided definitely to find out about accordions as soon as possible. She opened the box.

There, resting elegantly on a watermelon-pink rayon lining were a comb, brush and looking glass all made of pearly lavender stuff. Garnet was overwhelmed by their beauty.

"Oh Jay!" she said. It was all she could say.

"Okay, forget it," said Jay in embarrassment. "I

just thought you could use 'em. Come on, let's go into some of these tents and see what they've got."

They went into one tent after another. They saw Aurora, the Mystic Mind Reader, but didn't think much of her. "That's an old trick" scoffed Jay. "I could do that when I was nine years old." They saw Hercules Junior who was a chubby weight-lifter in a leopard skin and knee-high sandals. They saw Dagmar, the Sword Swallower, and she was wonderful and she *was* the same woman whom Garnet and Citronella had seen darning socks earlier in the day. They saw the Jewel Girls and Bruno, who were also perfect, and they listened to the orchestra of Hank Hazzard and his Hayseeds. "My eardrums feel black and blue," Jay said afterwards.

By that time it was getting dark and they went to gather their party together for supper. They had some difficulty in locating Mrs. Hauser, but finally found her at the shooting gallery taking aim at a tea-cup with one eye closed. They watched her demolish a whole row of teacups and some small statues, and receive with dignity the prize, which was an oil paint-ing of an Indian girl in a canoe. It had a frame made of real birchbark.

"Grandma Eberhardt will love this," said Mrs. Hauser. "She remembers Indians in Esau's Valley, and she's real fond of pictures anyway."

They all had supper together at a counter. It was Garnet's own party, and everyone had a good time. As they ate, the Great Zorander walked along his tightrope above the fair ground; a spotlight followed him and made his spangles glitter. He seemed a radiant and enchanted being as he moved with accurate grace so far above their heads.

Afterwards Garnet went to say good-bye to Timmy. The shed was full of flickering light and shadow cast by the oil lamps hung from the ceiling. Timmy staggered to his feet and sniffed at the palm of her hand. But there was nothing in it for him so he lay down again.

"Good night, Timmy," said Garnet. "In three days I will come and take you home."

Driving away in Mr. Freebody's truck Garnet turned and looked out of the window. The Ferris wheel was a ring of light, and all the tents were lanterns full of light. Among the dark, surrounding fields, the whole magical and temporary world of the fair glowed like phosphorus on a dark sea.

Citronella yawned.

"I don't think I'm going to want an ice-cream cone for a long, long time," she said.

X. The Silver Thimble

IT WAS a good thing that Eric had taught her to do handsprings and flip-ups, Garnet decided. It was very handy to know how to do one or two when you felt happy. Better than jumping. Better than yelling.

She went out of doors and did a few; then she remembered something that she had forgotten and went back in the house and up to her room. She rummaged first in a bureau drawer and then in her pocketbook, and took out the silver thimble. She rubbed it up and down, up and down, on the front of her Jersey till it had a good shine. Then she put it in the pocket of her sailor pants and went downstairs again.

Eric and Jay were nailing shingles on the roof of the barn. Except for the painting it was all finished, and very fine it looked.

There was a ladder leaning against it and Garnet scampered up and climbed onto the roof. Her bare soles clung to the shingles as she crawled up to the ridgepole where Jay and Eric were balanced like two crows.

"Hello," she said.

"You can help us nail shingles," said Jay handing her an extra hammer. She squatted down beside them, but she didn't do much work; she kept lifting her head to look about. Below was their own barnyard, with Madam Queen and her family in one pen, and Timmy in another. There was Brünnhilde, the black hen, scratching in her own little patch of ground; and nearby the other chickens, Leghorns, were behaving in the half-witted way that chickens do: scratching, pausing on one foot and shooting startled glances at nothing in particular, scratching again, and pausing, and clucking dreamily all the while.

Beyond the barnyard were the pastures; the cows were in one with all their heads bent to the grass; and in the other the horses galloped joyously in circles.

Beyond the Hausers' farm the river wound like a path made out of looking glass. All over the valley, as far as the eye could see, the corn had been cut and was stacked in wigwam shapes. The woods, still green on the hillsides were deep and shadowy, but everything else was the color of gold.

"Eric," said Jay suddenly, "what are you going to do when you grow up?"

"What I do now, just about," replied Eric promptly.

"I have it all planned. I'm going to work hard for your father as long as he'll let me, and save every penny I make. Someday maybe I'll get a farm of my own. In this valley I'd like it to be; near your father's and about the same size and style as his."

Garnet stole a glance at Jay from the tail of her eye. What would he say now?

"Eric, what do you want to be a farmer for?" he asked disappointedly. "There's no adventure to that; that's no way to see the world."

"I've seen plenty of the world, thanks" said Eric. "Plenty of adventure too, if you want to call it that. I like this better. I want to stay right here for years and years and years. And you know anyway, I like farming. Someday when I get one of my own, I'm going to have goats on it like my father did, and sheep, too, maybe. But I dunno, maybe not. Anyway I'll have hogs, and cows, and a team, but no hens except Brünnhilde, because she's the only one I ever saw that had some sense. Maybe I'll have just one rooster. A farm isn't a farm without a rooster to let you know when he feels the day coming."

"Aw, there's always trouble on a farm," grumbled Jay. "Blight, and stock diseases, and bugs, and drought."

"Drought!" said Eric scornfully. "That was a puny little drought you had here. You've never had trouble: you're darn lucky and you remember I said it. Why, I've seen rivers dried up and shrunk away to nothing, and the earth all full of cracks, and cattle dead for want of water. Yes, and in Kansas I've watched a wall of dust roll up from off the prairie black as your hat and high as the sky. We had to tie rags over our faces when it hit us, and even then it got into our eyes

133

and mouths. You felt it between your teeth, and down the back of your neck and in your pockets! After a few of those the farms that had been green and fine looked like the Sahara Desert. You don't know what trouble is, Jay."

There was a chokecherry tree that grew up out of the pigpen, and whose feathery top branches almost swept the roof. Jay leaned over and pulled off a sprig and chewed the bitter fruit reflectively.

"Well, I don't know," he said after a while. "Maybe you've got the right idea: but I still think I'd like to travel some, and see the world. But maybe when I got that out of my system I'd like to come back and farm with father. If you bought land next to ours we might work it all together and be partners and have a swell place. What do you think?"

Eric smiled with pleasure.

"It sounds okay to me," he said. "We'll all be partners; Garnet too if she wants."

Garnet felt pleased. She laid down her hammer and put her hands in her pockets. She found in one of them the silver thimble that she had brought to show Eric. She pulled it out and put it on her finger.

"Look Eric," she said. "I found this in the river on one of the mud flats that came up during the dry spell. It's solid silver and it's very valuable. You know why, Eric?" she leaned towards him and said defiantly. "Because it's magic, that's why. Jay says there's no such thing but he doesn't know. There *is* something wonderful about this thimble; everything began to happen as soon as I found it, why that very night the rain came and the drought was broken! And right after that we got money to build this barn, and you saw our kiln fire in the woods and came to be in our family. And then Citronella and I got locked in the library, that was exciting, and I went to New Conniston by myself. That was an adventure, too, even if I was mad when I started out. And then of course Timmy won a prize at the fair. *Everything* has happened since I found it, and all nice things! As long as I live I'm always going to call this summer the thimble summer."

"Well, if it's a magic thimble, I'm much obliged to it for bringing me here," said Eric.

Garnet was very happy. She was so happy, for no especial reason, that she felt as if she must move carefully so she wouldn't jar or shake the feeling of happiness. She descended from the roof cautiously, and walked with even steps down through the vegetable garden and across the pasture to the slough. A green light, tranquil and diffused, glowed among the willow saplings. The water was clear and motionless.

Garnet leaned against a tree. She was so quiet that a great blue heron, fancying itself alone, flew down between the branches and paused at the water's edge. She watched the handsome creature, with his blue crest and slender long legs, wading and darting his bill into the water. She was so near that she could see the jewel color of his little eye. He stood for a contemplative moment on one foot, still as a bird of carven stone; and in that moment it seemed to Garnet that he had become her companion; a creature who understood and shared her mood of happiness. For a second or two they stood like that in perfect stillness: and then the heron spread his heavy wings and flew away.

But now the happiness was growing out of all bounds.

135

Garnet felt that pretty soon she might burst with it, or begin to fly, or that her two pigtails would stand straight up on end and sing like nightingales! She could hold it in no longer. The time had come to make a noise, and whooping at the top of her lungs, she leapt out of the shadowy willow grove.

Griselda, the finest of the Jersey cows, raised mild, reproachful eyes and stared for a long time at Garnet turning handspring after handspring down the pasture.

NEWBERY MEDAL ACCEPTANCE SPEECH*

by ELIZABETH ENRIGHT

First of all, may I say that I feel both more proud, and more humble, than I have ever felt before. That you should have liked Garnet so much is as gratifying to me as if you had liked my own children.

Writing is still very new to me, and very exciting. My parents are both artists: my mother is Maginel Wright Barney, the illustrator, and my father is W. J. Enright, the cartoonist. One of my earliest memories is of being forcibly removed from my mother's studio, and afterward staring through the glass door at my mother, bent over her drawing board, ignoring me like grim death.

From the time that I was three years old and first began imitating my parents, I have always drawn pictures. I drew all over my schoolbooks, the telephone book, the blackboard, the sidewalk, my mother's best writing paper; and when I wore socks, I even drew faces on my bare knees. In fact, whenever I had a pencil in my hand, I was irresponsible and a menace.

It was not until I grew up and had illustrated several books that I began to think about writing. I don't suppose that I would have thought about it then, except that one day I found myself faced with a large, clean sheet of paper, and there happened to be a pen in my hand, so, as usual, I started scribbling pictures of peo-

*Read at the Children's Section meeting of the Sixty-first Annual Conference of the American Library Association in San Francisco, June 20, 1939, on the occasion of the 18th Award of the Newbery Medal.

ple. This time I made a lot of little boys; some were climbing palm trees like apes, some were throwing spears, and beating drums, and doing ceremonial dances. As I drew, a story began in my mind. I made a picture of a witch doctor in a derby hat, and then I tried a leopard or two. They were very bad. But by this time, I was intoxicated with a new idea. I thought how wonderful it would be to write my own book, and illustrate it exactly as I pleased.

So I elaborated on the theme of the little boy. First, I made all the pictures (like building a house beginning with the shingles). And then I bought a ruled pad and started to write the story. I tiptoed self-consciously through the first chapter, and I tore it up, and began again. After the first few crippling efforts, I was surprised to find that writing seemed to me an even more satisfactory means of expression than drawing. The finished result was a little book called *Kintu,* which was published by Farrar and Rinehart in 1935. I felt as though I had inherited the earth.

After this, I rested for two years, on laurels that were practically invisible, and wondered what to write about next.

One summer, I was in Wisconsin during a drought. I suppose that most of you have experienced a drought at some time or other, but this was the first one I had ever known. Each day we watched the grass grow drier and the oats turn yellow too soon. The air was full of a dry, sneezy dust, and the wind was like the breath of a blast furnace. It was a terrifying and infuriating thing to live with; nothing is so infuriating as weather behaving viciously, and you can't help feeling as though it had a grudge against mankind. You find yourself impotently hating it, and feeling offended.

Every evening about twenty of us would go down to the enormous vegetable garden with cans of water on the truck. Until the light failed, we toiled up and down interminable rows of vegetables, pouring water out of coffeepots and double boilers and anything else we could borrow from the kitchen. Afterward, our backs ached, and it hurt to unclose our fingers. But in spite of us, the corn withered, and the leaves shriveled away from the cucumber vines. All the green opulence of the valley turned sere and yellow before our eyes.

It was on one of the hottest days that I began the story about Garnet. It was a relief to describe and insult the outrageous weather, but I especially enjoyed writing about the thunderstorm which arrives just under the wire at the end of the first chapter. Unfortunately for us, though, in reality, the rain came too late and the valley didn't recover that summer.

It was a time I shall never forget. I am sure that anyone who has lived on a farm during a bad drought must carry the scar of it on his consciousness for the rest of his life. Like a vaccination.

From the first chapter about Garnet, I went on slowly building my book, *Thimble Summer* (this time properly from the foundations instead of the shingles). I remembered stories that my grandmother had told me about her childhood when that Wisconsin valley was a wilderness, and stories of my mother's school days in the same valley. I remembered incidents in my own experience, and pillaged the memories of my friends and relatives. The rest of it is my own. And I loved writing it.

There is a peculiar joy in writing about children *for* children. One naturally goes back to one's own childhood to find things. To me, the astonishing thing is in the way one took life during those years. It was as though a thin, but tough, membrane had not yet grown between oneself and the rest of the world. A child sees everything sharp and radiant; each object with its shadow beside it. Happiness is more truly happiness than it will ever be again, and is caused by such little things. The first day of spring, for instance, when it was warm enough to go without a coat; or the time you stayed up till nine o'clock, and someone showed you Scorpio, and the Pleiades, and Cassiopeia's Chair. Happiness came from the smell of a Christmas tree, or roast chicken on Sunday; it came from the first snowfall of the season, or learning to hang by your knees from a trapeze, or going barefoot in summer. I remember very well the glow of magic that illuminated the world for months after my mother had taken me to see Pavlowa dance; I remember the moment when my grandmother opened a book, and began to read me the first chapter of a story called *Treasure Island*.

Of course in every childhood there is sorrow, too. Sometimes a lot of it. And it seems more unjust and undeserved than it ever will again. Sorrow in childhood is a monstrous, alien thing, and one has not yet learned any philosophy that can dull the corners of it.

Fortunately, though, for the normal child who is brought up in safety, the grief lasts a far shorter time than the happiness. His grief is hot, and violent, and soon over, like a firecracker, but his unconscious joy and interest in living are steady, and taken for granted, as daylight is. Always, for him, there is the large, uncomplicated fact that he is loved, and protected, fed, disciplined, and dealt with justly by his family. The world, for him, is a secure, eternal place.

Let us all hope, even in such sick and troubled times as these, that someday it will be the privilege of every child to feel like this.